He Couldn't Den

Never before had he been ████████████████
And Chardonnay had been fully conscious of the
sexual attraction between them, even though in
the midst of a business battle they'd attempted to
downplay it.

As a plan formed in his mind, Spencer called his
attorney. "Find out which bank plans to loan her
the money and let me know immediately."

He'd have her—one way or another. Chardonnay
Russell would be his.

"Yes," he said through a smug smile. A marriage
for love was out of the question for Spencer. But
he'd certainly entertain the idea of a marriage for
lust....

Dear Reader,

It's hard to believe that *Spencer's Forbidden Passion* is my eleventh book in the Westmoreland series. Time sure flies when you're having fun, and I've really had a ball bringing you stories about these gorgeous Westmoreland men.

Spencer Westmoreland would be a challenge for any woman. Besides being too handsome for his own good, he's also smooth, suave and seductive. He believes in getting whatever he wants, no matter what it takes…and he really wants Chardonnay Russell! Will he succeed in charming the elusive Chardonnay? His quest to win her results in a red-hot, sizzling pursuit that I hope you will enjoy.

And if you like my Westmoreland men, I'd like to introduce you to the family that launched my career as a writer. I am pleased to announce the first titles in my Madaris Family and Friends series will be reissued. This month meet Justin Madaris, the ultra-sexy and unforgettable hero of *Tonight and Forever* (Arabesque Books). Please pick up a copy at a bookstore near you and find out why so many women are looking for a Madaris man of their very own.

All the best,

Brenda Jackson

BRENDA JACKSON

SPENCER'S FORBIDDEN PASSION

Published by Silhouette Books

America's Publisher of Contemporary Romance

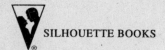

SILHOUETTE BOOKS

ISBN-13: 978-0-373-76838-7
ISBN-10:   0-373-76838-9

SPENCER'S FORBIDDEN PASSION

Copyright © 2007 by Brenda Streater Jackson

Printed in U.S.A.

BRENDA JACKSON

is a die "heart" romantic who married her childhood sweetheart and still proudly wears the going steady ring he gave her when she was fifteen. Because she's always believed in the power of love, Brenda's stories always have happy endings. In her real-life love story, Brenda and her husband of thirty-three years live in Jacksonville, Florida, and have two sons.

A *USA TODAY* bestselling author, Brenda divides her time between family, writing and working in management at a major insurance company. You may write Brenda at P.O. Box 28267, Jacksonville, FL 32226, by e-mail at WriterBJackson@aol.com or visit her Web site at www.brendajackson.net.

ACKNOWLEDGMENTS

To Gerald Jackson, Sr. Happy Anniversary!
Thanks for 35 years of love, happiness and romance.

To all my readers who joined me in April on the
Madaris/Westmoreland Cruise 2007. Thanks for making
it special, and this book is especially for you!

To my Heavenly Father. How Great Thou Are.

Let us go early to the vineyards
to see if the vines have budded, if their blossoms
have opened, and if the pomegranates are in bloom—
there I will give you my love.
—*Song of Solomon* 7:12

Prologue

"We've encountered a problem, Spence."

Spencer Westmoreland briefly closed his eyes to blot out two things—the look on his mother's face across the room and the frustrating sound of his attorney's voice on his cell phone.

He opened his eyes to find his mother was still looking at him with that, *I-wonder-who's-next* expression. He was in Bozeman, Montana, attending the wedding of his cousin, Casey, and his childhood friend, McKinnon Quinn. The couple was still inside the ranch house taking pictures. Everyone else who hadn't been a member of the wedding party was in the huge barn that had been miraculously transformed into a spacious ballroom for the reception.

He glanced around. Everyone seemed to be having a good time, smiling and happy. Everyone except him now that he'd been interrupted by a phone call from his attorney. Stuart Fulmer was one of the most competent men he knew, known for his precise and expeditious handling of all business matters, which meant if he felt there was a crisis then there definitely was one. "Okay, Stuart, what's the problem?" he asked.

"The Russell Vineyard."

Spencer lifted a dark brow and decided to step back into a corner of the room for privacy, as well as distance from his mother's intense gaze.

A few months ago he had gotten wind that the vineyard, located on over three hundred acres in the Napa Valley, was up for sale. He took the drive to the valley, saw it and fell in love with the area immediately. His research revealed that the owners, the Russells, were having financial difficulties and were struggling to hold onto the land. Spencer had sent his attorney to make the Russells an offer that had been more than generous. His plan for the property, once he became the owner, was to close down the winery and convert the place into a vacation paradise by adding a plush resort hotel and trails for hiking, biking and backpacking. It'd be the perfect tourist getaway.

The last he'd heard the negotiations were going smoothly and it would merely be a matter of days before the property became his. So what went wrong at this late date?

"What kind of problem are we talking about?" he asked abruptly.

"A young woman by the name of Chardonnay Russell."

He lifted a brow. "Chardonnay Russell? Isn't that the old man's twenty-seven-year-old granddaughter?"

"Yes, that's her. Somehow she has gotten the old man to change his mind."

Spencer frowned not liking the sound of that. "That's not acceptable. And I thought we pretty much had this deal wrapped up."

"We did."

"I also thought the Russells had a slew of money problems."

"They do."

"Then how can they afford *not* to sell?" he asked. When he noticed a couple of people who were standing around had turned to stare, he became aware that he'd raised his voice.

"They can't. But it's my understanding that she's making one last ditch effort to get the financing they need to hold onto the place. After all, it's been in the Russell family for over fifty years. I guess she's not ready for the family to throw in the towel just yet."

"That's admirable but too friggin' bad and too damn late. I want that property, Stuart. Do whatever you have to do to get it."

"It's going to be difficult, Spence. Chardonnay Russell isn't making things easy on my end."

Frustrated, Spencer rubbed a hand down his face. This was the first time in the fifteen years he'd known Stuart that he'd heard such aggravation in the man's voice. And all because of one female? Hell, how difficult could a single woman be? He then decided to find out for himself.

"Look, Stuart, let me handle things from here. I'll fly to Napa in the morning and meet with the Russells. Please let them know I'm coming."

He actually heard a sigh of relief in Stuart's voice. "I'm giving you fair warning to prepare yourself, Spence. The granddaughter may have been named after a wine, but there's nothing sparkling at all about her. Believe me when I tell you that she has the distinct sting of a scorpion."

Spencer couldn't help but grin at the words coming from the mouth of one of the most polite and mild-mannered men he knew. Chardonnay Russell must really be a handful. "Thanks for the warning. I'll keep that in mind."

One

"That man has arrived, Donnay."

Chardonnay Russell lifted her head and gazed into her mother's worried eyes. She tossed aside the pencil and notebook as she stood up. She hated to see her family agonize over money problems now. The winery had always brought in a substantial profit, but her grandfather's hospital bill earlier that year, and the subsequent cost of his medications had eroded their extra funds. Now they were barely hanging on.

So far every bank they had applied to for a loan had turned them down. Their last hope was the bank she had visited a few days ago in San Francisco. Mr. Gordon, the bank manager, had seemed positive and she had left in a better frame of mind.

"Donnay?"

The nervous tone of her mother's voice cut into her

thoughts. A smile played across Chardonnay's face as she crossed the room, not for the first time realizing her mother was a very beautiful woman. Donnay never knew her father. In fact, the only thing she'd been told about him was that her mother had met and fallen in love with him at eighteen. Chad Timberlain was a soldier on extended leave who had worked at the vineyards one summer and then returned to duty before finding out his short stay had produced a child.

"It's okay for him to wait, Mom. I'm sure it won't be the first time."

Or maybe it would be, she silently concluded. Earlier that day she had scanned the Internet to read up on Spencer Westmoreland. The thirty-six-year-old had made his first million before his thirtieth birthday. According to what she'd read, the wealthy tycoon had retired last year with more money than he could ever spend. Evidently he had gotten bored and wanted a new toy—her family's winery.

"Where's Gramps and Grammy?" she asked softly. She knew her grandparents were even more worried about their meeting with Mr. Westmoreland than her mother.

"They're in the kitchen. Janice has escorted our visitor to the study and he's there waiting."

Donnay nodded. "All right then. It's time for us to meet Mr. Westmoreland, and remember the three of you agreed to let me handle him my way."

Spencer paced the room and glanced at the various framed awards on the wall with a wry smile. Timing, he mused, was the reason he was being kept waiting. He hadn't become a successful businessman without knowing how the game was played. He was fully aware that the best way to keep a business opponent on edge was to make them wait. Stall them. Test their patience and their ability to endure.

He shook his head as an even broader smile touched his lips. The tactic was a waste of time with him, but Chardonnay Russell wouldn't know that. She had every reason to believe she was the one calling the shots and no doubt would be surprised to discover she wasn't.

"Sorry that you were kept waiting, Mr. Westmoreland."

Yeah, I bet, he thought, slowly turning toward the sound of the soft, feminine voice. Any further thoughts on his mind died a sudden death the moment his gaze connected to the most gorgeous pair of eyes he'd ever seen. They were silver-gray and he wondered if she was wearing colored contacts lenses, but quickly concluded she wasn't when he noticed the other three persons standing beside her had the same eye coloring. Evidently a family trait.

He quickly gathered his composure and said, "It was no problem."

The truth to the matter was that there was a problem and it came in the form of Chardonnay Russell. The woman was absolutely stunning. In his lifetime he had met and dated numerous beautiful women, but standing before him was definitely a rare beauty.

She was tall, at least five-nine. Slim and curvy in the short-sleeve white blouse and printed gypsy skirt she was wearing. And her facial features were exquisite. Dark, luxurious brown hair flowed around her shoulders. She had long lashes, mocha colored skin that looked incredibly soft, a perfect nose and kissable lips.

The hoop earrings dangling from her ears made her look even sexier. Made him feel hotter.

Never had Spencer's gut clenched so tight or every muscle in his body felt so taut because of a woman. But there was something flagrantly erotic about her, and while looking into her gray eyes all he could think about were satin sheets and entangled bodies.

"I think introductions are in order," she said curtly, slicing into his personal perusal of her and his lusty thoughts. He watched her kissable lips move; however, he wasn't listening. His thoughts were too centered on the alluring package she presented and how he would like opening it up, enjoying it.

"We have you at a disadvantage," she continued saying. "We know who you are, but you don't know us since we dealt with your attorney, Mr. Fulmer, in the past."

His gaze picked up her every movement when she crossed the room, giving him a chance to check out those long legs underneath her skirt as well as her small waistline. And to make matters worse, all it took was one sniff and he picked up her scent. The arousing fragrance only added to his inner frustrations. He had a natural ability when it came to business, but handling such an intense degree of lust was another matter.

"I'm Chardonnay Russell," she said, offering him her hand. "And this is my mother, Ruth Russell, and my grandparents, Daniel and Catherine Russell."

Spencer took Chardonnay's hand in his, and the moment their hands touched, an electrical current raced through him. The sensation annoyed the hell out of him and he tightened his jaw. This was not the time to be reminded that since he'd been extremely busy lately, he hadn't had a woman in over seven months. Unfortunately his increased heart rate was reminding him of that very fact and he was fighting hard to keep his features impassive, his mind sharp.

"Ms. Russell," he said, quickly releasing her hand. He then moved to shake the hands of her mother and grandparents. He noted her grandfather didn't look well and recalled reading in one of the reports that the winery's financial woes were due to the man's escalating medical bills.

"Now that introductions have made, please, let's sit down."

Chardonnay's voice cut into his thoughts, reminding him of why he was there. "Yes, I suggest that we do," he agreed.

"Like I've told Mr. Fulmer, the vineyard is no longer for sale. And I might as well warn you, Mr. Westmoreland, that if you assume you'll be able to change our minds about that then you are vastly mistaken," she said the moment she took her seat.

Spencer liked her spunk. She was definitely no pushover. "On the contrary, Ms. Russell. In business, one never operates on assumptions—at least not if one intends to be successful in getting what he wants."

He saw the quick frown that appeared around her eyes. Those same eyes he thought looked sexy as hell. "And you think you're going to get what you want, Mr. Westmoreland, even after I've said we no longer want to sell?" she asked, narrowing her gaze at him.

"Yes, I think so," he said rather arrogantly. "Mainly because you haven't seen my new proposal."

He couldn't help cutting her a very cocky grin, one he

was certain irritated the hell out of her. But at the moment he didn't give a damn. He was feeling adrenaline of another kind flow through his bloodstream. The one he always felt when pitted against a worthy opponent.

"Now," he said calmly, "I suggest you let me present a new proposal to you."

Donnay's head snapped up from the report she was reading. "What you plan to do with our land is unacceptable."

She saw the look in his eyes was tempered steel, and he didn't blink when he said, "It really shouldn't concern you what I plan to do with the property once I acquire it. All you need to be concerned with is that the price I'm offering is more than fair."

Donnay frowned. He was sitting across from her on the sofa, casually sipping the wine her grandfather had offered him before they got started with business. Some of Russell Vineyards' finest.

"Well, it does concern us, which is why we've decided not to sell. And now after reading this proposal I'm sure my family and I have made the right decision."

"If you think that, then you're wrong. Look at the proposal closely, Ms. Russell," he said in an annoyed tone, sitting up and leaning forward. "I'm willing to pay you a half million more than what I'd authorized my attorney to offer. I think that's more than generous and it's all the increase I'm willing to make. Can you and your family truly turn down the deal I've placed on the table?"

Donnay nervously bit her lip. Truly they couldn't. She didn't want to think about what could happen if the bank didn't approve their request for a loan. She glanced over at her mother and grandparents. They were depending on her to make the right decision for the family, especially her grandfather with his heart problems and diabetes. Still, she refused to let someone like Spencer Westmoreland waltz in and take advantage of their situation.

But then she should have known she was in trouble when she'd entered the room and he stood there, impeccably dressed in an Armani suit and looking like he was ready to buy or sell whatever suited his fancy. Then there were his looks that were sharp, sexy and suave. He had to be over six-three, with coffee-colored skin, short, dark hair, a generous mouth and the darkest pair of eyes she'd ever seen on a man. In fact, they were so intense that each and every time they connected to hers she felt a tingle slowly make its way up her spine.

"I asked you a question, Ms. Russell."

She glared at him, not liking his tone. She drew in an agitated breath as she glanced back over at her family. Her grandfather nodded and a slight smile touched his lips, giving her the encouragement she needed to give Spencer Westmoreland her answer. She had to believe that a miracle would come in the form of that friendly banker in San Francisco, who actually seemed sympathetic to their financial problems.

Taking such a chance might be foolish but, sighing deeply, she met Spencer Westmoreland's gaze and said, "Yes, we can turn it down and we will turn it down."

She then stood. "We've taken up too much of your time already, Mr. Westmoreland, and we have work to do around here. My family appreciates your interest in the Russell Vineyard but like I said earlier, it's no longer for sale."

Spencer stood and snapped his briefcase closed. He was silent for a long moment then he said, "If you think you've seen the last of me, you are sadly mistaken."

Donnay saw the smile that touched the corners of his lips when he added, "I'm finding you a worthy opponent, Ms. Russell."

She stiffened her spine. "Don't count on being a nuisance, Mr. Westmoreland. Just go find another vineyard to buy. And if you try making trouble for us, you'll be sorry."

His smile widened and the look he gave her sent shivers up her spine. "I promise I won't be the one making any trouble for you, but I can guarantee you that in refusing my offer, you've just made a lot of trouble for yourself. Good day."

Once Spencer had gotten at least a mile from the Russell Vineyard, he pulled the rental car to the shoulder of the road and placed a call on his mobile phone. He couldn't get out of his mind just how beautiful Chardonnay was and the degree of his attraction to her. Never before had he been so aroused by a woman.

He was intuitive enough to know that even with others in the room she had been acutely aware of him, just as he had been aware of her. And she'd been fully conscious of the sexual attraction between them, although in the midst of a business battle they had attempted to stay focused and downplay it.

"Stuart? This is Spence. I want you to find out which bank is leaning toward loaning the Russells the money and let me know immediately."

He clicked the phone shut and sat there for a long

moment, focusing on his surroundings. It was a gorgeous day for early December, and the land around him was beautiful. He wanted that land. A thought then flickered across his mind. In addition to the land there was something else he now wanted.

Chardonnay Russell.

His brows knitted together in deep thought. The single Westmorelands were dropping like flies, and from the look on his mother's face at McKinnon and Casey's wedding, she expected the next victim to be another one of her sons. So why should he disappoint her?

After Lynette Marie's betrayal, the thought of ever marrying for love was as foreign to him as a snowstorm in the tropics. He had mourned the loss of his fiancée, who had died in a jet-ski accident over four years ago in Bermuda, only to discover from the coroner's report that she had been six-weeks pregnant. That meant she had gotten pregnant sometime during the two months she had been there on business. That had also meant he had not been the father of her child.

His hand tightened on the steering wheel. A marriage for love was out of the question but he would definitely entertain a marriage for lust. Besides, at thirty-six he had accumulated a lot of wealth, wealth he had worked hard to acquire. It was time to think about his future and make some important changes.

Although he wasn't looking for a love match like three of his brothers, Jared, Durango and Ian, had been blessed with, it was time for him to settle down, marry and secure his future with a child who would one day inherit all of his wealth.

He couldn't help but smile when he thought of all the

babies born in the Westmoreland family just this year. His cousin Delaney and her husband, Sheikh Jamal Ari Yasir, had given birth to their second child, a girl, whom they had named Arielle. His cousin Dare and his wife Shelley also had a daughter born in August. Durango and his wife Savannah had been blessed with a daughter in September; and his cousins Thorn and Stone and their wives were expecting new additions to the family as well. Thorn and Tara's baby was to be born at the end of the month, and Stone and Madison were expecting their firstborn in February.

Spencer restarted the car's engine. As he continued the journey to the Chablis, the resort where he was staying, he knew the next time he and Chardonnay's paths crossed, he would be making her an offer. And this would not be one that she would refuse. He would make damn sure of it. He was now a man on a mission. He was also a man who was known to go after whatever he wanted and didn't let up until he succeeded in getting it.

And what he wanted with Chardonnay was a merger of the most intimate kind.

Two

"You have a phone call, Donnay."

Busy in the winery doing inventory, Donnay quickly turned and glanced at her mother, "The bank?"

Ruth shook her head, an anxious look on her face, "No, it's not the bank. I believe it's Mr. Westmoreland," she said handing her daughter the phone.

Donnay sighed deeply. Why hadn't her mother told the man she wasn't available? She was well aware that Spencer Westmoreland had gotten on her daughter's last nerve yesterday. "Thanks a lot, Mom," she said sarcastically, taking the phone. "Why didn't you tell him I wasn't here?" she whispered, placing a hand over the mouthpiece.

"But, his call might be important."

She rolled her eyes and gave a little huff under her breath. "I doubt it. The man just wants to harass me some more." She placed the phone to her ear when her mother left the room.

The last thing Donnay wanted to do was talk to the man whose image was still blatantly clear in her mind. Although she hadn't wanted to, she had thought about him after he had left yesterday, and even worse, she had thought about him last night. She had made the mistake of noticing how much of a man he was instead of concentrating on what a forceful, imposing individual he represented. That was one mistake she wouldn't make twice.

"This is Ms. Russell," she said rather gruffly.

"Ms. Russell, this is Spencer Westmoreland. I'm calling to ask if you would have dinner with me tonight."

Arousing sensations automatically flowed through Donnay's body at the seductive tone in his voice. She fought the feelings, not quite sure what to make of the man. She pursed her lips, trying to decide whether to hang up or continue the conversation.

She inwardly sighed before saying, "Mr. Westmoreland, why would I want to have dinner with you?"

"To save your family's winery."

Donnay's arched brow rose a fraction. "I hate to shatter your illusions but Russell Vineyards doesn't need saving."

"Are you absolutely sure about that?"

Donnay leaned back against a wine rack. No, she wasn't absolutely sure; especially since she hadn't heard back from the bank. Mr. Gordon had indicated he would let her know something by noon today. Although she felt fairly confident they would get the loan, she also felt it would be in her best interest to see what Spencer Westmoreland might have up his sleeve.

"I'm willing to listen to what you have to say. However, it doesn't have to be over dinner."

"For me it does. That's the way I conduct most of my business meetings."

Her words were edged with anger when she asked, "And what if I prefer not having dinner with you?"

"Then you don't get to hear what I have to offer."

Donnay tipped her head back. The man had offered a lot of money for the vineyard yesterday, more money than she or her family could have ever expected. "Do you not recall me telling you yesterday that we aren't interested in any offer you make?" she asked bluntly.

She could hear his soft chuckle and liked the sound of it. "I do, but I'm hoping that I can change your mind," he said.

"That's not possible, Mr. Westmoreland. Like I told you, the vineyard is no longer for sale."

"And you're willing to turn your back on my offer on the chance that some banker is going to come through for you?"

An intense degree of uneasiness prickled Donnay's skin. "What do you know about my dealings with any banker?" Her stomach churned as suspicion raised its ugly head.

"I merely assumed as much since a few weeks ago your family was desperate to sell the winery and now you're not. Besides, I make it my business to know the financial position of any potential business partners."

She didn't like the sound of that. "We aren't partners, potential or otherwise."

"If you want to believe that, go ahead. Now back to

dinner. We'll go to Sedricks. I'll be there to pick you up around six. Is that acceptable?"

She wished she could tell him that it was not acceptable, but as she stared out the window at the lush vineyard in the distance, she knew doing so might not be a smart move. She had no intentions of ever parting with the vineyard she was looking at, no matter how confident Spencer Westmoreland seemed to be. She had a feeling he was up to something and there was only one way to find out what. "Yes, six will be fine."

"Wonderful. I'll see you then."

As soon as he clicked off the line Donnay wasted no time contacting Wayne Gordon at the bank. Her stomach settled when he told her he had good news for her. The loan her family had applied for had been approved. Donnay felt happiness all the way to her toes. Spencer Westmoreland hadn't bested them after all. That remark he'd made earlier about her business with the bank had been meant to throw her off, emitting smoke when there really wasn't any fire. Their money worries were now over. She would pull out a bottle of their finest wine and her family would celebrate.

A smile touched her lips. She would take great joy in letting Mr. Westmoreland know she expected him to get out of their lives forever. And she couldn't think of a better opportunity to tell him than that night over dinner.

Spencer smiled as he settled comfortably in the back seat of the limousine he had hired for the night.

The call he had received earlier from Stuart had him in high spirits. Things were definitely going as he had planned. Thinking about the offer he would make to

Chardonnay later tonight sent heat all through him. The thought that he would be the one who made love to her with the full purpose of giving her his child practically had his loins on fire. Of course, not for one minute did he assume she would go along with his proposal.

His lips curved into another smile. There was no doubt in his mind that she would turn him down flat, fight him with every breath she took, which was why he intended to give her no choice in the matter. Not if she really wanted to retain possession of her family's winery.

He glanced out the tinted window, seeing the beauty of the countryside of the Napa Valley. He had fallen in love with California the first time he had visited over twenty years ago after accepting a scholarship to attend Southern California University. As much as he loved Atlanta, California had eventually become his permanent home. After obtaining a bachelor's degree in finance and then a M.B.A., he began a career in banking at one of the most prestigious financial institutions in San Francisco.

He loved going back home to Atlanta for family gatherings, but always looked forward to returning to Sausalito, the charming waterfront community that was located just across the Golden Gate Bridge. The town was often compared to the French Riviera because of its Mediterranean flair and breathtaking views.

His house, a distinguished looking two-story structure, sat on four acres of land with beautiful San Francisco and Bay views. But he had to admit there was something peaceful and charming about Napa Valley. Away from the hustle and bustle of traffic, it was an idyllic setting. The perfect place to settle down and raise a family.

His mind was set, his agenda clear. It was not in his nature to tolerate resistance when it came to meeting any of his goals. And this time would not be an exception.

Chardonnay stared at her reflection in the huge mirror, wondering why she was putting so much effort in looking good tonight, granted Sedricks was a very elegant and sophisticated restaurant.

She turned slightly and smiled. The strapless, backless black dress made of a sheer material clung to her hips, showing curves she had a tendency to forget she had until she dressed up in a manner such as this. She couldn't remember the last time she had gone out on a real date with a man. After that fiasco with Robert Joseph, her former college professor whom she had fancied herself in love with a few years back, she had a tendency to watch herself around men, especially those who thought they had it all together and expected women to fall in place and cater to their every whim.

She had been twenty-four and in her last year at UCLA, earning a degree in horticulture, when she had met Robert, a divorcé fifteen years her senior. The older man had dazzled her, swept her off her feet and into an affair that had lasted almost a year. A month before she was to graduate, he broke the news to her that he and his ex-wife had worked things out and were getting back together. She had realized then that she had been nothing more to him than a fun pasttime. The pain had taught her a valuable yet hard lesson when it came to men.

She tossed her head, sending her shoulder-length hair forward, framing her face. She grinned at the seductive effect and laughed. The rich sound vibrated in the room and made her realize it had been weeks since she'd had a reason to laugh. Almost losing the only home she'd ever known had taken its toll, but now she had a reason to rejoice.

"You look pretty."

She turned at the sound of her mother's voice and smiled. "Thanks, Mom, and I feel pretty tonight. I can't wait to tell Spencer Westmoreland that we have no reason to sell the vineyard, no matter how much he offers for it."

A worried look touched her mother's features. "Be careful, Donnay. It's my impression that Mr. Westmoreland isn't a man who likes losing."

She chuckled. "That's my impression of him as well, but I can't worry about that. How he handles bad news is no concern of mine."

"I know, but still, Donnay, he's—"

"Mom," she said, reaching out and grabbing her mother's hand. "Don't worry, I can handle Mr. Westmoreland." A smile curved her lips as she glanced at herself in the mirror again, thinking of the sheer arrogance of the man. "The big question of the night is can he handle me?"

Spencer slid out of the back seat of the limo when the chauffeur opened the door. He nodded, thanking the driver before walking briskly toward the huge house. When a cool breeze slid through his leather coat, he slipped his hands into the pockets in defiance of the crisp December air.

Although the sun had set and there was very little light, he could recall vividly the Russells's sprawling country home that seemed to loom out of the hills and sat on over a hundred acres of vintage land. Yesterday he had trekked this same path to the front door. The stone walkway, which seemed a mile long, was bordered with numerous flowering plants that seemed to welcome him.

Anticipation ran through his body with every step he took, and his heart began pounding furiously in his chest when he finally reached the door and pressed the bell. He tried ignoring the rush of excitement, thinking no woman had ever affected him this way, but then he conceded there was a first time for everything. And as long as he didn't let it dull his common sense, he could handle a little bit of craziness on a nippy December night.

The door opened and Chardonnay stood there, a vision of loveliness that practically took his breath away. His mouth pressed in a thin, hard line when he felt his common sense deserting him, and immediately he fought back the feeling. He liked being in control, but at that moment he feared that he was losing it.

She stepped back to let him enter. "It will take me only a minute to grab my wrap," she said, walking off.

His gaze sharpened when he saw her bare back. Her dress seemed perfect for her body and emphasized the svelte lines of her curves and the gracefulness of her long, gorgeous legs. The effect was stunning and he felt it all the way to his groin. He shifted, deciding it best to stay in place by the door, grateful for the full-length leather coat he was wearing.

He watched her grab her wrap off the table, place it around her shoulders and turn. Their gazes locked and at that precise moment, something passed between them. He felt it and was convinced she had felt it as well. Like him, she stood perfectly still, their gazes leveled, connected.

Then suddenly the sound of a door closing somewhere upstairs in this monstrosity of a house broke the spell, and she tilted her head and frowned at him. A deliberate smile curved his lips.

"Are you ready to leave?" he asked, deciding the sooner he got her out of this house, off this land and into the cozy confines of the limo, the better.

She nodded and he had a feeling that the smile she proceeded to plaster on her lips was just as deliberate as his had been. She crossed the room and, as graceful as a swan, came to a stop in front of him. "Yes, I'm ready."

As Donnay settled into the soft leather cushions of the limo, she inhaled the familiar scent of ripened grapes that drenched the night air. This was wine country. The hills, valleys, fields and meadows bowed to that very proclamation and had done so for years. She had been born here and they had buried a host of other Russells here on this land. This was her legacy. But even more importantly, this was her home.

Through the tinted windows and in the darkness her gaze still scanned the land the car passed. She was grateful she and her family no longer had to worry about losing what was theirs to someone who wouldn't appreciate the valley for what it was. Someone who wanted to destroy the land instead of wanting to cultivate it. Someone intent on turning what would always be a vineyard into a playground for the rich and famous. A vacation spot.

That very someone was sitting a decent distance from

her on the seat and hadn't spoken since the limo had left her family's home. She had to admit to surprise once she had walked outside and had seen the limo parked in the driveway. She should not have been. Spencer Westmoreland was a man who evidently enjoyed basking in his wealth.

In the dark interior of the car she allowed her gaze to scan his silhouette, bathed in the moonlight. He wasn't looking at her. In fact his gaze seemed fixed on the objects they passed; although she doubted he was actually seeing anything. That meant he was deep in thought, or just plain ignoring her.

The thought of him doing the latter should not have bothered her but it did. After all, he was the one who had invited her to dinner. She wondered if he'd already detected that this was one deal he'd thought he had wrapped up that he could now kiss goodbye. Not bloody likely. He was probably sitting there thinking of a new strategy to get what he wanted.

Hopefully after tonight she would make it clear as glass that her family would not entertain notions of selling the vineyard. She smiled thinking her mother and grandparents would certainly rest a lot better tonight. But when it came to how well she would sleep, she wasn't as certain. Not with the man sitting beside her on the seat causing all sorts of turbulent emotions to rise within her.

While he was looking elsewhere, she scanned his face. His features were sharp, as sharp as his arrogant tongue, a tongue he was holding tonight, thank goodness. But everything else about him was out there, in the open. He was handsome. That fact was a given.

Every single detail about his features—the rounded chin, the short dark hair, the full lips—contributed to a face that would make any woman take a second look. Then there was the way he fit his clothes. Yesterday she hadn't failed to notice he was a sharp dresser. No doubt beneath his leather coat was a designer suit.

"Have you been to Sedricks before?"

She blinked, realizing he had spoken. He had shifted positions in the seat and was staring at her. When had he done that? While she had been admiring his clothes? If that was the case, he hadn't missed her studying him.

Deciding she needed to answer his question, she said, "Yes, several times. Have you?"

"Once. I was impressed with both the service and the food."

"The food is wonderful," she said, suddenly wondering if they needed more space between them. For some reason it seemed the distance separating them had decreased.

"And that will give us a chance to talk."

She lifted a brow. "About what?" she asked, wanting him to get specific.

"A number of things." With a move that was so premeditated that it caught her unawares, he eased closer to her on the seat. Her heart rate escalating at an alarming rate, she glanced up at his face and fought back the panic she felt rising in her throat. She had made light of her mother's warning, however, when it came to experience, she was no match for Spencer. He had a sensuality about him that made the pulse in her throat twitch. Robert had been an older, handsome man who had impressed her with his intellect. But when it came to style, sophistication and fashion, he'd been slightly unkempt. He was a professor, and in his social circles and profession, one wasn't supposed to look like he belonged on the cover of GQ.

But it was a whole different story for Spencer West-moreland. He was a businessman, suave, debonair, hand-some…arrogant. Even now his presence was dominating the interior of the car. There was no doubt in her mind that in his world, his word ruled supreme. She doubted very few opposed him. And those who did probably paid the price. One didn't make it to where he was in life, and at such a young age, without being ruthless to some degree. Donnay shuddered at the thought. He wanted Russell Vineyards. She wondered how he would handle knowing it was no longer within his grasp?

She drew in a deep breath when he stretched his arms across the back of the seat. "I really wasn't sure you would go out with me tonight," he said in a throaty tone.

Her senses became focused fully on him when she said, "I'm a woman full of surprises, Mr. Westmoreland, and there's one I intend to share with you later."

"Is there?"

"Yes."

She saw his gaze study hers intently before he said, "You have beautiful eyes."

She could respond by echoing the compliment, but instead she decided to play it safe. "Thank you."

"You're welcome. You're also a gorgeous woman."

She slanted him a cool glance. It was on the tip of her tongue to tell him she was too levelheaded to fall for sweet talk. She wondered why he was wasting his time and couldn't imagine what he hoped to gain by using such flattery. It might work on other women but not on her.

"I must thank you for a second time, Mr. Westmoreland."

"Let's dispense with the formality. Call me Spencer."

She nodded. "All right, and I'm Donnay."

He smiled. "I like Chardonnay better."

She mentally shook aside the sexiness in his voice when he said her name. The scent of grapes, she noticed, had been replaced with the scent of man. Whatever cologne he was wearing was manly, robust and sexy. She knew for some woman he would probably be the perfect lover since there was no doubt he would be good at anything he attempted.

"Chardonnay."

She glanced up and saw his gaze was focused exclusively on her. She wondered what he was staring at so intently. Then she realized her lips had captured his attention and were holding it. She drew in a quick breath and felt a stirring begin in her stomach and slowly spread to all parts of her. And then there had been the way he'd said her name. Placing emphasis on certain syllables in a way no other man ever had, giving it an undeniably sensuous sound.

She parted her lips to draw in a much needed breath, and in a daring move he leaned closer and darted out his tongue to moisten her lips, before capturing her mouth with his. The contact had been so unexpected, so sudden, that instead of pulling away she felt every cell in her body vibrate under the onslaught of a combustible combination of overzealous hormones and much-deprived lust.

It was too late to revamp her senses. Too late to think about resisting. The moment his tongue touched hers she was a goner and she had a feeling that with his arrogant, utterly confident self, he very well knew it. What other reason could there be for him deepening the kiss and pulling her closer to him in such a way that had her moaning sounds she'd never heard before.

No man had ever kissed her this way. So completely, so totally, so downright absolutely. The kiss aroused her, stimulated her like none before. She responded to his actions on instinct and not experience. Her tongue had never participated in a kiss the way it was doing now, emanating a need within her that she didn't understand. But evidently he did, because the more she greedily demanded from him, the more he gave.

Suddenly he pulled back, and disappointment poured through her like cold water on overly heated skin. She noted she was draped over him, practically in his lap. And he was staring at her with an intensity that held both longing and possession. She knew at that moment, as she tried pulling herself back together and away from him, that she was out of her league. And to think she'd actually thought she could handle him.

"Your taste is one I'll never forget, Chardonnay."

She focused her full attention on him when he added, "And one I intend to indulge in time and time again."

His words were filled with confidence, as if barring any opposition or debate. By the same token, her reaction to them was immediate and instinctual. "I disagree."

He shook his head and smiled at her. It was a smile that touched his lips, corner to corner. "That's your prerogative. But the way I see things, your loyalty will be your downfall, but then at the same time it's what sets you apart from all others. It's what I admire most about you."

She frowned, not understanding what he was saying or what he meant. Before she could ask, he glanced out the car window and said, "We've arrived at our destination and I prefer resuming this discussion over dinner."

Three

Spencer knew he had selected the right restaurant the moment he led Chardonnay through the doors. The ambiance alone deserved the establishment's five-star rating.

Situated on a grassy slope in the heart of the Napa Valley, the huge European-style structure boasted elaborate stone and brickwork. The interior glistened with holiday decorations. Even on a Tuesday night the place was packed, and he couldn't help but note that more than a few males looked his way with envy in their eyes. More on instinct than anything else, he entwined his arm with Chardonnay's. When she gave him a questioning look, he smiled and said, "I made reservations so we shouldn't have long to wait."

No sooner had he said the words then the maître d' appeared to escort them through the throng of well-dressed patrons to a private room in the back of the restaurant. Brick walls with dark wooden beams and cast-iron chandeliers that hung overhead created a romantic setting.

After being seated at the only table in the room they were given a wine list and their menus. They were informed that a waiter would arrive shortly to take their wine selection and dinner order.

Moments later he was alone with Chardonnay. Spencer glanced up at her face, trying to read her expression as well as guess her thoughts. He knew he had surprised her when he had touched her arm with such possessiveness. Hell, he had surprised himself. Never had he been jealous of another male's attention to any woman he was with. It wasn't in his makeup to do such a thing.

Giving himself a few moments to clear his rattled mind, he followed her gaze around the room. It was quaint and cozy, almost completely surrounded in tinted glass, and it provided a beautiful illuminated view of an outdoor gazebo that was surrounded by thick shrubs, blossoming flowers and running vines.

"The room is lovely."

Chardonnay's comment caught his attention and he met her gaze. It was on the tip of his tongue to say that the room had nothing on her. "Yes, it is," he said instead. The taste of her was still on his lips and he doubted even the strongest drink would be able to remove it. He had enjoyed kissing her, sliding his arms around her and holding her close to him while he mated with her mouth at will. And when her arms had wrapped around him, and he'd heard the soft moans from her throat, he had done what had come naturally. Deepen the kiss even more.

Not that he was complaining, but the intimate

exchange had lasted longer than he had intended. All sense of time and place had flown from his mind in the awakening lust that had consumed his body. And when she had stretched up against him, he had effortlessly pulled her into his lap without disengaging their mouths.

His thoughts came to an abrupt end when the waiter brought in glasses of water and then took the time to take their wine and dinner order. They both agreed on a veal dish and a bottle of Russell Chianti.

"Have you ever tasted our wine before?" Chardonnay asked after the waiter had left, leaving them alone again.

He shook his head. "No, but I understand it's delicious."

She frowned. "It's more than delicious. It's superb. The best in the land."

He chuckled. "You would say that but I'll see for myself in a minute." He then leaned back in his chair. "What exactly do you do at the winery?"

She shrugged. "A little bit of everything, depending on the season. I handle PR during the winter months—spring and summer I work the vineyard, pruning, planting and I even know how to operate the equipment to crush and ferment the grapes. In the fall I take on the role of wine taster. So I guess you can say I enjoy wearing several different hats."

After taking a sip of her water, she asked, "Why are you interested in what I do?"

He smiled, wondering if she was always so suspicious of people or just him. Then again, she had good reason to be. "Um, just curious."

She placed her glass down and met his gaze. "And I'm just as curious, Spencer," she said, leaning forward and saying his given name for the first time. "What is tonight all about? Why did you invite me to dinner?"

He leaned forward as well and countered by asking in a low, husky voice, "Why did you accept?"

She slowly drew back and lifted her chin. "Because there was something I wanted to tell you."

"What?"

She inclined her head toward the closed door. "I prefer we wait for our food, especially the wine, since what I have to say is a cause to celebrate."

He lifted a brow. "Is it?"

"Yes, I think so."

"All right then. In the meantime tell me about yourself."

He immediately saw defiance light her gray eyes before she said. "I already have. It's your turn."

Spencer started to say she was wrong. She hadn't told him everything about herself. Since she would eventually become his wife, he had an urge to know a whole lot more. However, he said, "I'm a Westmoreland."

The smile that touched her lips stirred something deep in the pit of his stomach. "And that's supposed to mean something?" she asked, seemingly amused.

He shared her smile and felt rather comfortable in doing so. "In Atlanta it does. Just like your family has deep roots here, mine has deep roots in Atlanta. My cousin Dare is sheriff of College Park, a suburb of Atlanta. And my cousin Thorn Westmoreland is—"

"The man who builds motorcycles and races them as well," she finished for him, smiling brightly. "I didn't make the name connection until now. I used to have a poster of him on my bedroom wall when I was sixteen. Boy was he hot."

Spencer chuckled. "I understand there are some women who think he still is. He's happily married, and he and his wife, Tara, are expecting their first baby later this month. It's going to be a boy."

"That's wonderful. And what about siblings? Do you have any?"

"Yes, I have an older brother, Jared, and four younger brothers—Durango, Ian, Quade and Reggie."

"They all live in Atlanta?"

"Jared and Reggie do. Ian lives in Lake Tahoe and Quade works for the government in D.C."

"Really, what sort of work does he do?"

"Quade works in security at the White House. Because of the high level of security entailed, we're not really sure what he does and he's never divulged any details." And so she wouldn't ask any more questions about Quade's job, he asked a question of his own. "What about you? Is it just you, your mother and grandparents?" he asked.

"Yes, and the four of us are very close."

"And your father?"

She shrugged. "I never knew him and he never knew me. End of story."

Spencer knew it was the end of the story only because she deemed it to be. At that moment the waiter returned with their wine. After he filled their glasses and left the room, a smiling Chardonnay held hers up for a toast. "To Russell Vineyards, may we last forever, and with the loan we got approved today from the bank, we are well on our way of doing just that."

She glanced at him over the rim of the glass as she then took a sip, smiling. Spencer knew she was feeling really good right now, thinking she had just burst his bubble.

She lifted a brow as she put her glass down, evidently disappointed that she had failed to get a rise out of him. "Well?"

He lifted his own brow. "Well, what?"

"Don't you have anything to say?"

He smiled and then replied, "Yes, I have quite a lot to say, but I prefer to do so after we enjoy our meal. I wouldn't want any words we might exchange to ruin our dinner."

Apparently thinking she *had* succeeded in getting him riled after all, she leaned back in her chair and said smugly, "You'll get over it."

"And if I don't?"

He watched as she drew her breath, saw how her lips curved in a frown. She leaned forward again. "It will be a waste of your time since there is nothing you can do about it."

The waiter entered with their food. Spencer smiled at her and said, "Our dinner has arrived, Chardonnay. Please hold your thoughts until after our meal. Then I will tell you why you're wrong."

Donnay declined dessert, thinking she was tired of this cat-and-mouse game she and Spencer were playing. During the drive over, she had felt elated, confident, thrilled at the prospect that he would be experiencing a letdown like he hadn't felt in a while, given what she had read about him. He should be totally disappointed, frustrated and probably more than a little upset to learn Russell Vineyards was completely out of his reach. Instead it didn't appear that the news had affected him at all, which made her wonder if perhaps he knew something that she didn't.

And then there was the kiss she couldn't get out of her mind. The one that still had her insides sizzling. His lips had connected to hers in a way that immediately set off a rush of heat within her. And the chemistry that had been stirred between them was as potent as anything she'd ever felt before. His taste had literally zapped her of her senses and it was taking everything she had to get her entire body back on track.

Not able to handle the tension or curiosity any longer, she tilted her head up and looked into his face. "Tell me why you think I'm wrong, Spencer."

She watched him set aside his wineglass. He then eased his wallet out of his jacket pocket and withdrew a business card. He offered it to her.

Donnay took it, studied the information that was printed on it before looking back at him with a questioning look. "What am I supposed to be looking at?"

"My profession."

She glanced at the card again before raising her head to meet his gaze. "Financial management investor?"

"Yes. Like you, I enjoy wearing several different hats," he said, putting his wallet back in his pocket.

Donnay sat straighter in the chair. Their gazes held for a long time when she finally asked, "Meaning what?"

Spencer continued to hold Chardonnay's gaze. There was no doubt in his mind that she wouldn't like what he was about to say. She would probably like even less the proposal he intended to offer her. For a fleeting instant he thought of undoing all he'd done; let her and her family keep the land and just walk away. He knew that although he could walk away from the land, he could not walk away from her. Spending time with her tonight had only solidified his interest, attraction and desire. He wanted her with a passion unlike anything he'd ever known.

He met her eyes as intently and said, "Earlier you said your family had managed to secure a loan."

"Yes, it's been approved."

"I know it has."

"And how would you know that?"

When he didn't answer her right away, she repeated the question. "How would you know that, Spencer?"

He leaned back in his chair. "Banks offer loans to individuals that sometimes have to be underwritten by a third party because of their risky nature."

He gave it a few moments and then he saw the light that came on in her eyes, letting him know she was finally getting the picture. That same light suddenly flared with fury when she asked. "Are you saying you're the one who underwrote the loan?"

He answered her, deciding to speak slowly and deliberately, making sure she understood completely. "Yes. The bank couldn't find any other investor to do it. So basically, once you sign the loan papers I'll be the one holding the mortgage to the vineyard."

His words had the effect he knew they would. Her eyes hardened and began shooting fire at him. "You want our land that much?" she asked in a tone he knew she was trying to control.

He decided to be completely honest. "Yes, but there's something else I want, Chardonnay, and it has become even more important to me than Russell Vineyards."

"And what is that?"

He only paused a second before saying, "You."

* * *

It took Chardonnay a few moments to gather her composure. And she couldn't help inhaling a deep breath several times before asking what may have been a relatively stupid question. "For what purpose?"

He took his time in answering her. "I want to marry you and give you my child. In fact, several of them."

She gasped first in surprise, then in outrage. "Do you honestly think I will go along with a notion as crazy as that?"

"Yes. You will if you want to keep your family winery," he said, looking her straight in the eye. "Evidently you don't fully understand your family's predicament, Chardonnay. Without the backing of a third party, no bank will agree to loan you the amount of money your family needs. You've depleted a lot of the business assets, not to mention you continue to be a mom and pop operation that has been operating in the red most of this year. However," he continued, "I'm willing to guarantee the loan for whatever amount you need. And to show what a generous person I am, I'm giving you two options. You can take out the loan but it will have to be paid back in full within six months."

"Six months!"

"Yes. If you default on the loan, everything will be mine. Or you can consider the second option. Agree to marry me and have my child and I will let you continue to run and operate the winery as you see fit. In fact I will put a lot of my money behind you to expand the winery to an international one."

Anger swept through her. Neither were acceptable options. She leaned over and glared at him. "Forget both options."

He gave a small nonchalant shrug. "If that's what you really want. But either way, Chardonnay, I will own your land one day and will do whatever it takes to do so. I suggest you take the second option. It's less risky. And if you do, I will even forgo my dream to build the vacation resort on the land. Instead I will devote my time and attention, when I'm not trying to get you pregnant, to building up Russell Vineyards' reputation and standings."

"I will not be your brood mare!" Donnay stood, amazed at just how much anger she could feel toward one single individual. "You have to be the vilest man I know to suggest something so despicable. The last thing I'd want is to marry you. And as far as having your baby, I can't imagine the two of us ever sharing a bed to do such a thing."

"Are you saying that you're willing to walk away from everything I'm offering knowing the outcome?" he asked in a calm voice.

"Walk away and not look back. Take note, Spencer Westmoreland, because that's just what I'm doing. And don't worry about taking me back home. I'll call a cab."

And then she did just what she'd said she would do. With her head held high she turned and left the room. And she did so without looking back.

When Spencer caught up with Donnay outside the restaurant, she was thanking one of the valet's for calling her a cab. "I'm taking you home, Chardonnay," he said, coming up behind her.

She swiveled and the look she gave him would have turned lesser men to stone. "No, you're not. I refuse to have anything to do with you, and if you try forcing me to do anything against my will, I will let out a scream the likes of which you've never heard before."

He believed her. "Very well, then," he said quietly, taking a step back. "But there is one thing I'd like to ask."

"What?" she all but snapped.

"Forget about the vineyard for a moment and all the things my proposal entails. I want to know what is there about me that rubs you the wrong way."

Donnay shook her head. The man really didn't have a clue. Did he not know how degrading his offer was to her? He wanted to marry her and use her to have his child. What could possibly be romantic about that? The sad thing about it was that she wanted the very things he was proposing—marriage, babies, a way to take the winery to an international scale. But not this way and definitely not on his terms. What he was proposing only showed just how ruthless he could be and how far he would go to get anything he wanted.

She tilted her head up and looked him dead in the eye when she said, "The reason I can't conceive of the two of us ever coming together romantically, Spencer, is that personally, you are *not* my type."

"Miss, your cab has arrived."

The attendant's words claimed Donnay's attention. She hurried over to the parked cab, leaving Spencer standing there alone.

"How was dinner with Mr. Westmoreland?"

Donnay glanced up at the stairs at the sound of her mother's soft voice. She could not tell her mother or grandparents the true nature of her evening with

Spencer. The last thing she wanted was for them to worry about anything.

"Dinner was okay," she said as she watched her mother descend the stairs.

When her mother reached the bottom stair, Ruth smiled at her and said, "It was just okay? I've never known a time that I went to Sedricks that the evening ended up being just okay."

Donnay smiled back at her mother. "Well, considering the company, it was just okay."

"And?" Ruth probed.

Donnay lifted a brow. "And what?"

"And how did he handle the news that we had secured a loan?"

"Better than I wished he had, giving me the feeling that he won't give up," Donnay said, admitting that much.

"Well, considering everything, how much ruckus can he stir? Getting the loan puts him totally out of the picture now since we won't need his money."

"Let's hope so," she said guiltily in response to her mother's words. She wished she could be completely honest and tell her mother that Spencer and the loan were tied together as one. The first thing she would do tomorrow would be to visit with Glenn Forbes, their attorney. She was certain Spencer had done something unethical in the handling of the loan. If fighting him legally was the only way then she would do so.

Needing to change the subject, she glanced at what her mother was wearing. It didn't take much to tell that her mother, who rarely went out, had gone somewhere tonight. "And where have you been?" Donnay asked, curious. Years ago, she had stopped encouraging her mother to get out more, meet a nice man, have fun and date, since her mother claimed there would never be another man in her life she could possibly love more than she had Donnay's father.

"McClintock Café," her mother answered. "After you left I got a call from a friend I hadn't seen in ages who was passing through. We got together for coffee and to catch up on old times."

Donnay nodded. It was good seeing her mother taking interest in something other than the winery. "Well, I'm glad. You look nice."

Yawning, her mother said. "Thanks. And I believe we're both up later than usual and need to go up to bed. The next few weeks will be busy ones for everybody."

The winter months were usually less hectic. Except for winter pruning, there wasn't much to do but take precautions to assure that the sometimes harsh weather didn't cripple or destroy the crop. It was also a time for staff members to discuss how to increase productivity and retain quality.

But a couple of weekends from now, downtown Napa would be hosting the annual Taste Napa Downtown event, which for wine lovers was the most popular wine tasting event in the world. Russell Vineyards would be represented again this year.

"Yes, and I can't wait. The excitement is spreading already," Donnay said, giving her mom a hug. "Good night, Mom."

"Good night, Donnay."

Donnay was halfway up the stair when her mother called out to her "Donnay?"

She turned. "Yes?"

Her mother stared at her for a moment then shook her head and smiled. "Nothing, sweetheart. At least it's not anything that we can't talk about later."

"You're sure?" she asked, studying her mother's features to detect if something was wrong. When she couldn't identify anything, she relaxed her brow.

"Yes, I'm sure. Go on to bed and get a good night's rest."

Donnay smiled. "I will and you do the same."

Four

You are not my type…

Irritation lined Spencer's brow as he took a sip of coffee. He couldn't imagine any woman saying such a thing to a Westmoreland. And if Chardonnay thought for one minute her words would stop him for acquiring the single most important thing he wanted—namely her—then she needed to think again. But still, what she'd said had irritated him, although he didn't have to speculate on the reason she'd said it.

He took another sip of coffee. He didn't care what she claimed, especially when her lips had said differently. He might not be her type but she had enjoyed the kiss they had shared. There was no way she could convince him otherwise. And he couldn't help wondering if memories of being in his arms had kept her awake last night as they had him. In addition to her beauty, there was something so beguiling about her that he hadn't been able to take his mind off her, even when he'd slept.

And that wasn't good.

With a frustrated sigh he pushed away from the table and stood. How could he have become so mesmerized by one woman? And so quickly. Even now the scent of her still lingered with him. It was such an arousing fragrance, one he couldn't let go of. He had left his cousin's wedding with the intent of coming to California to turn a deal around. Instead he was the one getting turned around. The woman was having just that kind of effect on him. He wanted to marry her. He wanted her to have his children. He wanted it all, and as far as he was concerned, no one else would do. On the other hand, he didn't expect this to be any sort of love match. Everything was strictly a business affair.

However, she had made it pretty clear, business or otherwise, she wasn't interested. He would turn up the heat a little, because in the end, he very much intended to have every single thing that he wanted, especially her. And he wasn't someone who wasted time once he'd made up his mind. He glanced at his watch. It was almost noon and time for him and Chardonnay to have another talk.

Less than an hour later he was strolling up the walkway toward the Russells' front door. He refused to entertain the notion that considering how they'd parted the night before, Chardonnay would refuse to see him. Whatever it took, he would get her alone so they could talk.

He was halfway to the door when suddenly it was flung wide open and Chardonnay's mother appeared, frantic, almost hysterical with tears streaming down her face. "Mr. Westmoreland, please come quickly! Help us. It's my father. He's collapsed and is unconscious."

"Are you saying there's nothing that we can do, Glenn?"

Glenn Forbes had been the attorney for Russell Vineyards for years and Donnay was trying hard not to let the man see her frustration.

"Unfortunately that's exactly what I'm saying," the sixty-something year-old man answered. "It will be Westmoreland's money that he's loaning out so he can set up any terms and restrictions that he wants. And chances are, he will be giving you stiff ones since the bottom line is that he wants your land."

"How stiff?"

"He will probably call in the loan during a time he knows you can't possibly pay it back, or hike your interest rates up so high that you'll have difficulty making the loan payments, which will ultimately push you into defaulting. On the other hand, if you don't take the loan and he's the only one interested in buying the property or if he keeps the same offer on the table that he made a few days ago, then you and your family will make a lot of money."

"But we'll lose our home." She sighed deeply, knowing Spencer had backed them into a catch-22 situation. Either way he stood to gain and they could lose everything that truly mattered to them. "Thanks for the information, Glenn."

"No problem. How's your grandfather's health?"

Donnay smiled. "It's been good. His medication is expensive but we've been able to handle it so far. He's a little disappointed that we've had to put aside our plans for expansion for a while. Right now our main focus is surviving."

For years her grandfather, who was the master wine-maker in the family, had worked hard to improve the quality of the wines they made. Although Russell wines had a great reputation in the United States, the next stage in their plan had been to start doing business in the overseas market. That meant hiring more employ-ees, some with specialized winemaking skills. That was one of the reasons Spencer's offer to transform the winery from a mom-and-pop operation to an interna-tional one had merit. It was the same plan her grandfa-ther had been dreaming of for years. But the price Spencer demanded was too high.

She stood. "Well, I need to be going, Glenn. I've taken up too much of your time already."

"Nonsense," the older man said, also standing. "Just be careful with those city slickers like Westmoreland. He'll take advantage of any mistake you make. If he wants that land bad enough he'll do just about anything to get it."

Donnay didn't need to be warned. She already knew how far he'd go. She gave Glenn a small smile and was about to make a comment when her cell phone went off. Pulling it from her purse she checked caller ID. "Excuse me, Glenn, it's Mom calling." She flipped open the phone. "Yes, Mom?"

Seconds later she grabbed the edge of Glenn's desk for support when a lump of panic swelled within her throat. "What! How is he?"

She nodded anxiously. "I'm on my way."

"Is anything wrong, Donnay?"

She glanced up and met Glenn's concerned expression right before she quickly headed for the door. "Yes, it's my grandfather," she said to him over her shoulder. "He collapsed and had to be rushed to the hospital."

Donnay rushed through the E.R. doors and looked around frantically for her mother and grandmother. Relief washed over her when she saw them, but tension and anger quickly consumed her when she saw who was with them.

What was Spencer Westmoreland doing here? Was he responsible for whatever was happening to her grandfather? Had he said something to upset him? Her grandfather had been perfectly fine when she had eaten breakfast with him that morning, long before her mother and grandmother had awakened. And now he was here in the hospital.

Inhaling deeply and trying to consume the anger she felt, she crossed to where the three individuals sat. Spencer was the first to see her and stood after whispering something to her mother and grandmother. They glanced up and rushed over to her.

"How's Gramps?" she quickly asked.

"We don't know," her mother responded softly. "The doctor hasn't come to talk to us yet. Everything happened so fast. We were all in the kitchen. He was fine one minute and the next thing we knew he was clutching his chest and then he collapsed."

"There's a possibility he had a heart attack," Spencer said when he joined them.

Donnay's eyes locked with his. Rage consumed her. "And what do you know about any of this?"

Her mother answered. "He was there to—"

"He was there!" Donnay broke in as her anger escalated even more. "What did you say to my grandfather? You had no right to upset him. If anything happens to him I will never forgive you."

"Donnay, you're wrong. Mr. Westmoreland—"

"Sorry your opinion of me is so low, Chardonnay," Spencer cut into her mother's words. "And since my being here has upset you, I'll leave." He turned and quietly headed toward the exit.

Ruth grabbed her daughter's arm, highly disturbed. "What is wrong with you, Donnay? Why would you talk to Mr. Westmoreland that way?"

"I can't stand the man. You know that, Mom."

"Yes, but it was a blessing that he showed up when he did today or your grandfather might not be alive."

Donnay was too stunned to speak. After a moment she asked in an unsteady voice. "What do you mean?"

"After your grandfather collapsed, I was rushing out of the house to get one of the workers when I saw Mr. Westmoreland coming up the walkway. He ran in and administered CPR to your grandfather until the paramedics arrived. He was not responsible for what happened to your grandfather. Instead of sending that man away, you should have thanked him. What you just did was incredibly inconsiderate."

Donnay knew she looked as totally embarrassed as she felt. The floor could open up and swallow her whole and she would deserve it. "Mom, I didn't know. I truly thought he was responsible."

"I don't know why you would think such a thing. You owe him an apology."

Before she could respond, they turned when the doctor walked into the waiting room. Donnay rushed over to him. "How is he, Dr. Miller?"

The older man, who had been her grandfather's doctor ever since it was discovered that he had a heart condition earlier that year, gave them a small smile. "He's resting and, yes, he did have a heart attack. One that could have taken him out of here had it not been for the quick thinking to use CPR. As soon as he's stable we want to run more tests. That surgical procedure we discussed a few months ago would help tremendously although most insurance companies won't pay for it since it's still considered experimental in nature."

"Can we see him?" her grandmother asked softly.

"Yes, but one at a time and for no more than five minutes. It's important that he continues to rest."

It was only after her grandmother's and mother's visits with her grandfather that Donnay entered his room. She had seen him like this before, hooked up to various machines and monitors, but seeing him now profoundly affected her. In her eyes he had always been strong, robust and bigger than life. Now he appeared tired and weak.

She walked quietly across the room to stand beside his bed. She gazed down at him, remembering years when he represented the only father-figure in her life. She couldn't think of losing him, like she had refused to let him consider losing the one thing that meant everything to him, other than her grandmother—the vineyard.

When the family hadn't been able to see through their

financial situation, he had been willing to part with the one thing that had been in the Russell family for generations, although she'd known doing so was killing him inside. She'd known then that it would be up to her to make sure he'd never have to do that. That burden was still on her shoulders.

"Donnay."

She blinked back tears when he opened his eyes, met her gaze and said her name, barely murmured under his breath. "Yes, Gramps, I'm here."

"Pretty."

She smiled. He'd always told her she was pretty. She watched as he tried moving his gaze around the room and knew why. "Grammy and Mom were here earlier. They will only let us see you one at a time."

He nodded, letting her know he understood. "I'm nothing but trouble."

She frowned upon hearing his words. "No, you're not, so don't even think that. Everything is going to be all right."

He looked up into her face. "The winery?"

She felt a thick lump in her throat as she nodded and brushed moisture off his forehead. "The winery is going to stay with us. We got approved for the loan, remember?"

He nodded again and a slight smile formed on his lips. "We're going to keep it."

She blinked back more tears. "Yes, we're going to keep it."

"For your kids."

A smile touched her lips. Even in his condition, he was again dropping hints about her personal life. "Yes, one day for my kids."

"My great-grands."

"Yes, Gramps, your great-grands." She watched as his eyes closed. He was dozing off again, apparently being tired out from talking to her.

"Miss, I hate to interrupt but your five minutes are up," a nurse stuck her head in the door and said, smiling apologetically.

"Thanks, I'm leaving." Leaning over she placed a kiss on her grandfather's cheek, then clutched the shoulder strap of her purse as she left the room.

Spencer stared down into the dark red depth of his wine before swirling it around in the glass. Russell Vineyards' finest. Last night Chardonnay had referred to it as superb and he had to admit she was right. He'd never had a reason to taste the wine before last night but now he was mildly surprised. He hadn't expected such a fruity, yet tartly smooth taste. He found it incredibly pleasing to his palate.

Instead of sipping he put the glass to his lips and thought, what the hell. He had ordered it. Room service had delivered it. And at the moment, he needed it. He took a rather large gulp and then licked his lips while the warmth of the liquid flowed straight through his body to settle in a part of him right below the belt.

Seemingly sensual. Definitely erotic.

It was then, and only then, that he took the time to fully recall every vivid moment of the scene that had played out at the hospital with Chardonnay. A hard muscle twitched in his cheek. She had wrongly accused him, but instead of defending himself, he had walked away. He had discovered last night that once Chardonnay became upset about something, the woman was downright hard to deal with … even when her facts were wrong.

But unlike his attorney, Stuart, he had no intentions of letting her test the level of his endurance or get on his last nerve. After all he still intended, whether she liked it or not, to marry her. She just wasn't making things easy for him, which meant he would continue to make things hard for her.

He crossed the room to gaze out the window in an attempt to calm his frustrated mind. The abundance of land his eyes touched was incredible, amazing, simply beautiful. The sun was sending golden highlights across the valley in a way that was astounding and peaceful.

As if to break that peace, his mind went back to Chardonnay. He loathed the very idea that she thought he would intentionally bring her grandfather harm. If she knew how much he had cherished and loved his own grandfather, she would know how totally wrong she was. Scott Westmoreland had made an impact on all of his grandchildren's lives, making them believe that they could fulfill their dreams, no matter what they were. Like Chardonnay's grandfather, he had been a master, not at wine but at food. His reputation as a cook and restaurant owner was legendary. And Spencer had loved him as deeply as Chardonnay loved her grandfather.

He turned away from the window when his cell phone rang. Thinking it was Stuart or one of his brothers, he answered. "Yes?"

"I owe you an apology."

Spencer felt a deep tingling in the pit of his stomach the moment he heard Chardonnay's voice. There was just something incredibly sexy about it. However, the effect it had on him was too intense for his frame of mind, and resentment set in. For a moment he didn't know what to say since he never expected her to call to apologize. "Do you?" he finally replied in a clipped tone.

"Yes."

"I'm sure it's something you don't do often. Do you really know how it's done?"

There was a slight hesitation on her part and then she said in an irritated tone, "Look, I don't need this."

He'd gotten her mad. Good. "And neither do I, Chardonnay. I don't like being falsely accused of anything."

"I told you I was sorry. What else do you want?"

"Have you decided to indulge me in the things I want?" he retorted coolly, waiting for her response, knowing it would probably be just as biting and sharp as his had been.

"You have got to be the most—"

"Be careful what you say, Chardonnay, or you might very well be apologizing for a second time." He was taunting her and he knew it. She had pushed a number of buttons that no other woman had pushed before and he didn't like it.

"I think we need to end this conversation," she said brusquely.

"I don't. The reason I was at your home earlier today was that I felt we needed to talk. I still feel that way," he said.

"Maybe some other time."

"No. Tonight."

For a moment she didn't say anything and then asked, "And if I refuse?"

"Then either way, you can kiss the winery goodbye." He had said the words calmly, but Spencer was fully aware she knew he meant them.

"One day you'll regret what you're doing."

She was probably right but as long as that day wasn't today he was fine. "We'll do dinner at seven, here at the resort. I'm staying at the Chablis." He also knew his words probably sounded like an order.

An incredulous smile touched his lips when he heard the sound of the phone clicking in his ear. That wasn't a dropped call. She had deliberately hung up on him.

Hours later, Donnay murmured not so nice things about Spencer under her breath when she headed down the stairs. Spending time with him again was not something she wanted to do. The less she saw of the infuriating man the better. However, she had to admit that they did need to talk. She just didn't want to do it tonight.

"There you are," her grandmother said smiling. "I was just about to come up and get you. The car has arrived."

Donnay lifted a brow. "What car?"

"The one Mr. Westmoreland sent for you. It's parked outside."

As soon as her feet stepped off the bottom stair Donnay walked over to the window and looked out. That same limo from the night before was parked outside. Why had he sent a car for her? Spencer said they would be dining at the Chablis, the luxury resort on two hundred acres of land that overlooked the Mayacamas Mountains and provided a stunning view of Napa Valley.

She turned to her grandmother wondering if she knew what was going on.

"Is Spencer outside waiting in the parked car, Grammy?"

"No, he sent his driver for you. The man came to the door to let us know he was here, and said he'd been instructed to take you to Mr. Westmoreland at the Chablis."

Donnay looked outside again at the limo and shook her head. The man really did have a lot of nerve. She turned back to her grandmother. "I'm using my own car."

She walked across the room and gave her grandmother a peck on the cheek. "I'll have my cell phone on if you need me."

They had already checked with the hospital and her grandfather was still resting peacefully. Her grandmother had wanted to spend the night with him but they had talked her out of it.

Donnay glanced around. "Where's Mom?"

"She went out."

Again? Donnay lifted a brow. Evidently that friend her mother had met for coffee last night was still in town. "Will you be okay here alone, Grammy?" she asked with concern.

Her grandmother waved off her worries. "Of course. Go on and enjoy the evening with your young man."

Donnay frowned, doubting that she would. "Well, if you're sure you'll be okay, I'll go and let the limo driver know I'm taking my own car."

"All right, dear."

Grabbing her purse off the table Donnay quickly walked out the door. She strolled down the long walkway to the chauffeur and smiled up at him. "Hello, I'm Chardonnay Russell, and I won't need your services since I'm driving my own car."

The man's face remained expressionless when he said, "Mr. Westmoreland instructed me that if you were to refuse my services, madam, to give you this," he said, presenting a sealed envelope to her.

Frowning, she took it from the man, quickly opened it up and pulled out the note.

I prefer that you do things my way, Chardon- nay. For your safety, comfort and convenience, I have sent the car for you and I expect you to use it. Failure to do so means all talks are off, includ- ing my backing that loan. Spencer.

A part of her wanted to say good riddance, but she knew she couldn't do that, especially after she had assured her grandfather today that all was well with the vineyard.

Keeping her irritation in check, she glanced at the driver and gave him a small smile. "It seems I'll be using your services tonight, after all."

Five

His dinner guest had arrived.

A semblance of a smile danced across Spencer's lips as he reached for his jacket on the back of the sofa and put it on. He'd figured that Chardonnay would refuse to ride in the limo so he had taken the necessary steps to deny her a choice. It might have appeared underhanded on his part but he could not entertain thoughts of her driving back home alone late at night.

The moment the limo came to a stop, he walked out the front door of the two-story cottage he was occupying. Standing in the doorway he watched the driver walk around the front of the impressive shining black automobile to open the rear door. The windows were tinted so Spencer couldn't see Chardonnay, which he figured was just as well since chances were she wasn't too happy with him about now. She was a woman who didn't like being told what to do, especially when he was the one doing the telling.

He continued to watch as the chauffeur presented her his hand and she stepped out of the car. Tonight she was wearing her hair up and several strands had escaped confinement and were curling around her face. To his disappointment she was wearing a pair of slacks, which meant he wouldn't be ogling her legs tonight. Too bad, they were such a stunning pair, too gorgeous to be hidden.

His senses remained locked on her every movement and when she glanced his way, a frown settled on her features. He was tempted to cover the distance separating them and kiss that frown right off her face. Instead he continued to stand there, portraying an expression of nonchalance when he felt anything but.

Seeing her again was having one hell of an effect on him, an effect he was struggling to control. Lust in itself was a killer, a yearning of the worst kind. But when you mixed it with obsession, especially one that kept you from thinking straight, you were in deep trouble. The bottom line was that he wanted her. At almost any price. However, she would be the last person to know since that kind of information in her hands would be tantamount to lethal.

"Glad to see you arrive in the car I sent, Chardonnay," he said when she began walking toward him. He tried deciphering her mood and quickly reached the conclusion that she was definitely not a happy camper.

"Did I have a choice?" she asked curtly when she stopped in front of him, tilting her head back to look directly into his eyes.

"No," he said simply, truthfully, before moving aside

to let her enter. It was either that or be done in by the turbulent depths of the stormy gray gaze that narrowed at him. His restraint not to reach out and pull her into his arms to smooth her ruffled feathers was weak.

"I thought we were having dinner."

She was standing in the middle of the living room, glancing around. Evidently she had expected to see a table set for two and had noted there wasn't one. He moved toward her, deliberately slow, fighting back the urge to let his gaze slide over her from head to toe. She looked good in her black slacks and a turquoise top. The shade, he thought, complemented her coloring. Since the evenings and nights in the valley could get rather chilly, she had brought a tweed jacket, which was slung over her arms.

"We *are* having dinner," he said. "But I didn't want the food to get cold before you arrived. It won't take long for room service to set things up, and I hope you enjoy the entrée I ordered for us."

She glared at him. "And if I don't?"

She was itching for a fight and he sure as hell had no intentions of obliging her. He was getting used to her moods. Besides, he would be calming whatever storm was brewing inside of her soon enough. Therefore, he responded to her question with a dispassionate shrug and said, "Then I suggest you don't eat it."

He saw the way her lips tightened into an even deeper frown. "Do you always manage to have things your way?" she asked coolly.

"On the contrary," he replied, thinking if that was true she would be in his bed this very moment.

"There are some things I find myself doing without,"

he added, sliding his hands into his pockets so he wouldn't be tempted to reach out and pull her into his arms, capture her mouth beneath his, and touch her all over. The thought of doing any of those things had his heartbeat accelerating.

To counteract the effect, he nodded toward the huge window and said. "So, what do you think of the view?"

She followed his gaze and an unexpected smile touched her lips, making his guts clench. "It's beautiful," she said with something akin to spellbinding awe in her voice. "But then this is home for me and I've always thought the valley was the most exquisite place to live."

"I'm beginning to believe that, although I love my home in Sausalito."

She turned back around, and met his gaze with an arched brow. "You live in Sausalito?"

"Yes. You sound surprised."

"I am. I thought you would prefer the fast pace of San Francisco instead of the quietness of a small town."

He chuckled. "I grew up in a fast-paced town—Atlanta. I always wanted to live someplace peaceful and serene."

"I'm surprised such a thing doesn't bore you."

"I'm sure there's a lot about me that would surprise you, Chardonnay."

Her expression was one of indifference, and a part of him was determined to change that. "Make yourself comfortable while I call for dinner."

She didn't verbally acknowledge what he said. Instead she moved toward the sofa and sat down. He felt perspiration form on his brow while watching her graceful movement, appreciating the way her hips swayed, the slender curves of her body.

Deciding he needed to do something with his hands, he picked up the residence phone. "This is Spencer Westmoreland. You can deliver dinner now."

"When will we talk, Spencer?"

She asked the question the moment he'd hung up the phone. He met her gaze, saw the gray glint that was still ready for combat. His pure male persona was fighting an inner war not to put his plan of seduction in place before it was time. "We'll talk after dinner," he replied.

She reluctantly nodded and he knew that he would need as much strength as possible, because in dealing with Chardonnay Russell, only the strongest would survive.

Donnay drew a long, deep breath as she tried to keep her eyes off Spencer. It was hard. He had received a phone call and she'd been glad for the slight reprieve. Now she had time to study him without him being aware that she was doing so. He was rich, powerful and suave, and dressed in a pair of expensive trousers, a designer white shirt and a smooth-cut suede blazer, he definitely looked the part of a millionaire.

In addition to all that, he was magnificently built: tall, strong and masculine. The perfect male specimen. His very presence was causing emotions to flood her that were better left alone. The man was a predator. He was ruthless and lethal all rolled into one, but at that moment she thought he was the most desirable man she had ever come close to knowing. With a snap of his fingers he could destroy her and her family's livelihood. And she couldn't let that happen. What she wanted, what she needed to know was why he wanted to marry her. Why he wanted her to have his children. The man was as rich as he was good-looking, so finding a woman to fulfil his every need shouldn't be a problem. So why her?

"I just received good news from home," he said, hanging up his cell phone and reclaiming her thoughts.

She mentally shook off seeing the smile on his lips, the one that sent blood rushing through her veins. "And what is the good news?"

"Thorn and Tara's son came three weeks early."

"Is he okay?"

Spencer chuckled. "The baby and Tara are doing fine. However, I'm not sure about Thorn. I just finished talking to him and I think he's still in a daze. He was there with Tara during the delivery and said it was an awesome experience."

"I'm sure it was."

He didn't say anything for a moment, but his features held a pensive look. And then as if he'd made his mind up about something, he crossed the room and halted directly in front of where she sat on the sofa. "That's what I want, Chardonnay."

Donnay met his gaze. As far as she was concerned the man wanted a lot of things and it was hard to keep up. "And what is it that you want?"

He stared at her for a moment and then said. "I want to be there when my wife gives birth to our child."

To her surprise, his voice was gentle. Her senses registered his sincerity. And the look in his eyes was intense. Too intense. It was actually sizzling her insides. She hadn't expected that and lifted her head, narrowing her eyes. "Then I suggest you let the woman you intend to marry know that."

"That's precisely what I'm doing."

His gaze had her entire body feeling hot. "Don't fool yourself about that," she tried saying in a calm voice. "I am *not* the woman you're going to marry."

"Can you afford not to be?" he asked smoothly, cool and controlled.

She refused to let him back her against the wall any further. Her back stiffened. "You would use my family's land to force me into marriage with you?"

She watched his mouth hardened around the edges. "Yes, and I wouldn't hesitate doing so."

"And you would marry me, knowing I would despise you for it?"

He nodded. "Yes, because I'll put forth an extra effort each and every day to make sure you would eventually get over it."

She opened her mouth to give him the blasting retort she felt he rightly deserved when there was a knock at the door, indicating their dinner had arrived.

Chardonnay's fragrance was getting to Spencer. It was an arousing scent that made him think of everything other than the half-eaten steak on his plate. The food had been delicious. But then he figured, so was the woman sitting across from him. He wanted Chardonnay with a passion that, until now, had been foreign to him.

During his lifetime he'd never allowed himself to be swept away by passion, infatuation or obsession. He hadn't done that with Lynette Marie and he'd been quite taken with her. At least he'd thought so at the time. They had met and dated in college, and after graduating they had gone their separate ways, each wanting to devote time to their chosen careers.

Hers had been in broadcasting and she had immediately landed a job at CNN as a television journalist. They had renewed their relationship almost ten years later after bumping into each other while both had been in New York on business. Afterward, they began a long-distance romance, which had worked for the both of them, lasting a couple of years. When he'd felt the time was right, he had asked her to marry him and she had accepted.

A few months after announcing their engagement, she had gone to Bermuda on a three-month assignment. Unfortunately, with his busy work schedule, he never got a chance to visit with her while she was there. Then one morning while shaving, he'd gotten a phone call from her parents informing him of her accidental death.

The coroner's report had indicated that at the time of her death she was six weeks pregnant. Spencer had known the child wasn't his since they hadn't made love in over four months. Her betrayal left him determined to never share his emotions with a woman again. And he had sufficiently heeded that decision…until now.

Inwardly frowning, he lifted his gaze and looked over at Chardonnay from across the table. Other than inquiring about her grandfather's health and other mundane small talk, they hadn't said much during dinner; however, she seemed to be enjoying her meal.

Deciding they had put off the reason she was there long enough, he said, "Now we'll talk, Chardonnay. But keep in mind we need to stick to the important issues, and I want your decision in forty-eight hours."

She narrowed her gaze at him. "You can't expect me to make up my mind that soon."

"Yes, I can and I do. And I won't change my mind

about it. I refuse to give you time to drum up alternatives that I won't go along with. All you'll be doing is wasting both of our time. I presented the two options to you last night. Do you have anything you want to ask me about them?"

"Yes," she said, setting down her wineglass. "If we agree on the loan, what limits and restrictions will you be placing? And what happens if we miss a payment?"

He leaned back in his chair. "The interest rate will be higher than the present market and if you miss a payment, I'll begin foreclosure proceedings before you can bat an eye."

He had been brutally honest and from the look on her face she hadn't liked his answer. He was intentionally making the loan unattractive and blatantly risky.

He watched her hesitate a moment, fiddling with the food on her plate before lifting her head. Her stony-gray eyes met his dark ones when she asked in a curt tone, "This marriage of convenience you want. Just what would you expect of me?"

A smile touched his lips when vivid visions flooded his mind, some so blatantly sexual they made him ache. "I would expect of you what any man would expect of his wife. I want to sleep with you every night, make love to you, get you pregnant—several times—and provide a home for you and our family."

She hesitated again, and then asked, "And after I've ceased being of any value to you?"

He mused, surprised by the question. "Why would you think a time would come when you'd cease being of value to me?"

From the expression on her face he could tell his

question confused her, so he decided to ask another. "Just how long did you assume I wanted our marriage to last, Chardonnay?"

She shrugged her shoulders. "Until I had given you all the children you wanted."

He threw his head back and laughed. "Then what was I supposed to do with you after that?"

"Divorce me."

He arched an eyebrow upon realizing she was serious. "There hasn't been a divorce in the Westmoreland family since before I was born. In our eyes, marriage is sacred."

Donnay frowned. "Are you implying that you expect us to stay together *forever*?" she asked with disbelief in her voice.

"Yes, till death do us part. Why wouldn't that be the case?"

He could tell his question caught her off guard. "Because most marriages of convenience are for a set period of time, and usually a rather short one."

"Ours won't be. But I need to make sure you understand that love will not be a factor in our relationship mainly because it won't have a place in our marriage. I don't need it and personally I don't want it."

He paused, wanting to make sure she understood what he was saying. When he continued speaking, his voice was slow and his words were chosen carefully. "If you agree to marry me, you'll be agreeing to a loveless marriage, basically a business arrangement between us. I will treat you with respect and bestow upon you everything that comes with being my wife."

"Except love," she interjected.

He nodded. "Yes, except love."

She didn't say anything for a brief moment. "And if I go along with marrying you, what guarantee do I have that you will give up the idea of turning the winery into some vacation resort?"

"There aren't any guarantees other than my word. And I will give it to you now. If you agree to marry me, Chardonnay, you and your family's financial worries will be over. I will turn my attention toward three things. Getting married, getting you pregnant and doing whatever it takes to escalate the winery to an international scale. I agree that Russell wine is superb and I will put my money into making sure the entire world knows it as well. I will help build the vineyard into something that we can one day pass on to our children."

"Why?" she asked quietly. "Why is getting married and having children important to you all of a sudden?"

He lifted a brow. "What makes you think my wanting those things is a sudden urge?"

She met his gaze. "Because you would have them already, if you truly wanted them."

He wouldn't admit to her that he'd always wanted children. In fact, that was the main reason he had asked Lynette Marie to marry him. But after her death he had eradicated a family from his agenda... until the moment he had seen Chardonnay. Even now the thought of spending time with her in bed, getting her pregnant with his child, made him hard.

"I'll be thirty-seven in less than six months and over the years I've accumulated a lot of wealth. It's wealth I want to pass on to my offspring and I need a wife to do it," he said.

"No, you don't," she argued. "Men get women pregnant without marriage on their minds all the time." He couldn't help but wonder if she was thinking about her own father since he obviously wasn't in the picture.

"That's another Westmoreland rule," he said with strong conviction. "We take responsibility for our actions, no matter what they are. The only woman I ever intend to bear my child is the woman I'm married to."

His heart began beating like an insistent drum when he watched her push her plate away, signifying that dinner was officially over. He stood and walked over to the phone and called room service to come clear away their plates and to bring them another bottle of wine from Russell Vineyards. After that was done he leaned against the counter and said, "Now I have a question for you."

Her gray eyes flickered his way.

"I know about your involvement with that professor a few years back. Are you involved with anyone now?"

He watched as a dark color stained her cheeks and he could tell that once again she had been caught off-guard by one of his questions. She probably felt outrage in knowing he had dug into her past, knew her personal business. "Don't be bothered by the question, Chardonnay. Like I told you before, I make it my business to know everything there is to know about any business partner, and that's exactly what you and I will be if we choose to marry. Partners. There won't be any secrets between us."

"Would it matter?" she all but snapped. "It appears I don't have any secrets you don't know about anyway."

"No, you probably don't," he agreed quietly, thinking he'd let one woman do him in with her secrets and blatantly refused to let such a thing happen again. "You never did answer my question as to whether you're involved with anyone now."

She glared at him. "You seem to know everything there is about me. What do you think?"

He slowly strode over to the table to stand in front of her. "It doesn't matter what I think, Chardonnay. It's what I want to know, what I want you to tell me, what I want to hear from your own lips. And if I ever find out you've deceived me, there will be hell to pay and the Westmorelands will have the first divorce in the family in over fifty years."

A sudden knock on the door announced the arrival of room service. Deciding to let her sit while his words sank in, he moved away toward the door. Minutes later, after the hotel staff had cleared the table and left, they were alone once more and he had no intention of letting her not answer the question he had asked earlier.

Seconds turned into minutes before she finally gave him an answer, after releasing what he considered a frustrated sigh.

"No, I'm not involved with anyone."

He took a step back, satisfied. A smile touched the corners of his lips. "That's good to know, especially considering what I'm about to do," he said, removing his jacket.

She frowned. "And just what are you about to do?"

He glanced at her. "Prove you wrong. I intend to show you that I am most definitely your type."

Six

Donnay quickly got to her feet. "You will do no such thing!"

She stared at Spencer, wondering if he had lost his mind…and at the same time wondering if she had lost hers, when desire began heating her entire being. She gritted her teeth, refusing to give in to what she was feeling, what was trying to take control of her impeccable good sense.

"Why shouldn't I get the chance to prove I am your type?" he asked, taking off the cuff links to his shirt. "However, if you want to go ahead and concede that you're wrong—"

"I am not wrong!"

"Then prove it," he countered. "Or rather let me prove otherwise."

She held her ground, though she could feel herself

start to tremble. With fear…or desire? "I don't intend to let you prove anything, Spencer."

"That means you either don't know your own mind or you're afraid of what I'm capable of doing to that mind."

The latter was true and in acknowledging that fact, a sensuous shiver rippled down Donnay's spine. Their kiss last night had done things to her she hadn't expected. It had literally blasted her world into another hemisphere. Another kiss might be even more lethal than the last and she had no intentions of playing with fire. Seeing him now, standing there, staring at her with his intense dark eyes, was making her entire body flush with some sort of feminine heat she'd never encountered before. The room suddenly felt hot and she felt hot right along with it and wondered if she was running a temperature. The Spencer Westmoreland kind.

"Do you know what I think? What I truly believe?" he asked in a deep, husky voice that set her body throbbing.

She met his gaze. He was standing in the middle of the room, his legs braced apart in a sexy stance, with his hands in the pockets of his trousers, staring at her with an intensity that nearly made her weak.

"No, and I couldn't care less what you think or believe, but I'm sure you're going to tell me anyway," she said curtly, just as angry with herself as she was with him. Why was he the one man who could cause such conflicting emotions to rip through her?

"I think you're a very passionate woman."

Passionate? Her? He had to be kidding. If he was basing his opinion on what had happened the other night he was way off. Although Robert had never complained, to be quite honest, she never found sex to her liking. It was all right, but definitely nothing she couldn't do without. In her mind it was a process intended to make bodies sweat and give your muscles a fairly good workout. Nothing more, nothing less, and she was okay with that. But then, she couldn't explain what was happening to her now. She didn't think what she was experiencing had anything to do with passion. It was more akin to lust.

"I think you have me mixed up with someone else," she decided to say. "Either that or you've drunk too much wine and it's screwed up your brain."

He didn't respond and she eyed him as he bent over to remove his shoes and socks. "May I ask what you're doing?" she inquired. He straightened up and kicked his shoes aside.

Another smile touched his lips. "I told you what I'm doing. I intend to prove to you that I'm your type."

She placed her hands on her hips. "Evidently you didn't hear me when I said that you're not doing any such thing, and I don't take you as the type of man who would force himself on a woman."

He smiled. "I'm not, but if a woman begs, then—"

"Beg? The only thing I'll beg is your pardon. Do I look like a woman who would beg a man for anything?"

"Not yet."

He slowly began walking over to her, like a hunter cornering his prey. But she refused to back up. He intended to prove her wrong and she intended to show him she was right. He was cocky, ruthless, domineering…all the things she never liked in a man. Therefore, he wasn't her type. Men like him turned her off.

Usually.

So why not now? Why was the hard glint in his eyes daring her to look away, making certain parts of her body feel hot, wet, and amazingly charged? And why was she suddenly remembering the kiss they had shared last night? The one that had had her purring, had made her want to press closer to him, feel every inch of him against her. The one that compelled her to drape herself over him, find her way into his lap while he claimed her mouth in a way no man had done before.

He came to a stop in front of her and then stood there, almost body to body, face to face. "You're remembering last night, aren't you?" he asked, breathing the words against her mouth in a way that nearly moistened her lips.

"No, I'm not remembering last night," she denied.

"Then how about letting me jog your memory?" he said. At the same time he reached up and tenderly caressed her cheek with his fingers.

She forced the lump back down in her throat, the one that was almost responsible for the soft purr that threatened to come out. She was beginning to forget everything, especially just how much she didn't like Spencer. Instead she stood there and stared into his eyes in heated fascination while intense sensations flooded her stomach.

"Do you know I could actually taste you in my mouth all day?"

She licked her lips nervously, thinking Robert had never told her anything like that the day after they'd kissed. And when Spencer's fingers left her cheek to caress the underside of her right ear, she couldn't think at all. She swallowed and forced herself to speak, although the voice that came forth didn't really sound like her own. "Can we talk about something else?"

He chuckled, and she watched how the smile lines spread from one corner of his lips to the other. "Sweetheart, to be quite honest, we really don't have to talk at all. In fact I prefer that we didn't."

Donnay knew what was coming next and tried taking a deep breath to prepare for it, but nothing could have prepared any woman for the mouth that suddenly swept down on hers, taking it, capturing it while at the same time a sweet and delicious tongue danced inside.

Instead of resisting, she met him and let him lead. She thought he had the flavor of peppermint, but the tang of man. A part of her felt a deep need to savor both. Her mind wasn't prepared for this, although it seemed her body was. When she felt his arms wrap around her, pulling her body closer to the fit of his, she became aware of the way the hard, toned muscles of his abdomen complemented the lower part of her body, further stimulating its feminine heat.

In some part of her mind it registered that his hands had moved from her waist and had begun a journey, exploring every inch of her body within their reach. But she was too preoccupied to get caught up in what Spencer's hands were doing. She was too busy drowning in the warm scent of his cologne, and the way his tongue was melding to hers.

Suddenly, however, she did become aware of his hands again when they inched down the back zipper of her slacks and slowly went inside the waistband to touch bare flesh. Her skin sizzled beneath his caress; her entire insides began throbbing. His hands were made for a woman's pleasure. They were manly, yet soft to the touch.

A part of her couldn't believe this was happening or

that she was letting it happen. It was as if she'd given up any willpower she had, giving him the liberty to latch onto her mouth, to taste her senseless, to touch her in a way that had a rush of heat flooding her body. Never had she experienced a kiss so intimate, pleasurable, one that had her insides tingling all the way down to her toes. Beneath the onslaught of his mouth she felt breathless, weak in the knees, consumed with desire.

She suddenly realized Spencer had slid her slacks down to her knees and was gripping the bare flesh of her behind that the thong she was wearing didn't cover.

She felt herself slowly falling, then realized that wasn't the case, it was Spencer easing her down onto the sofa. And, as if it had a mind of its own, her body became supple, receptive and nonresistant in his arms. When she felt the soft cushions at her back she opened her eyes and looked up into his at the same time he pulled his mouth away to slip a hand beneath her head. His face hovered above hers as he shifted their bodies to a more comfortable position and lay half propped over her.

Her heart began beating at an alarming rate and the urgency she felt within her couldn't be held at bay. Their faces were close and their gazes were locked. She detected his change in breathing the same moment she detected her own.

Slowly he leaned forward, softly whispered her name before capturing her lips, playfully nibbling, licking and sensuously torturing them with his tongue and teeth. What he was doing elicited a fierce reaction from her and she closed her eyes against the sensations ripping through her, fearful of losing her sanity.

And then he was kissing her again, even more in-

tensely than before, sweeping her away on a turbulent storm that made a guttural moan escape her lips. And just like before, she kissed him back, needing the taste of him, wanting to be physically close to him. She would probably regret all of this later, but for now, she accepted what she wanted and what she needed.

Drugged by desire, she returned his kiss with a passion and hunger she hadn't known till now. In his arms she turned brazen, wanton. Only Spencer had the ability to rob her of common sense and replace it with something so addictive she couldn't think straight.

The moment she felt cool air hit her skin, she realized he had lifted her blouse, and before she could give a moan of protest, he moved his lips from her mouth to undo the front clasp of her bra with his teeth. The moment her bra fell open and her breasts escaped confinement, he was there, greedily taking one into his mouth, his tongue lavishing pleasure of the most erotic kind.

Then she felt his hand ease inside her thong and possessively clutch her feminine mound just seconds before his fingers stroked her, making her wetter than she was before. She moaned out his name although she tried holding it back.

What he was doing to her down south, coupled with his mouth on her breasts up north was having one tremendous effect and she felt herself floating on a sensuous wave. Nothing she and Robert had done had ever escalated her to this degree of passion. This was foreplay at its finest and experiencing this kind of intimacy nearly shattered her brain cells. She closed her eyes, thinking she'd been dead wrong. He was her type in more ways than one. He was sharing with her the kind of passion she hadn't known she possessed. Forbidden passion. Hidden passion. He was exposing it and making her aware that not only did it exist but it was his for the taking.

And then he shifted his attention to her other breast while his fingers remained between her legs relentlessly stroking her. She opened her eyes, willing her strength back, but she felt as though she was drowning in delicious waves that were completely overwhelming her, possessing her, forcing her to acknowledge his power over her.

He finally let go of her breast and before she could say anything, he captured her mouth again. He interwove his tongue with hers, mated thoroughly, extensively, completely.

Suddenly he pulled back rested his forehead against hers, breathing in deeply. She had a feeling that like her, he was fighting hard to reclaim a normal heartbeat, which wasn't easy. Moments later he looked down at her, and she felt herself falling deeper into the intensity of his gaze.

"Tell me," he whispered hotly against her lips. "Tell me you were wrong and that I am your type, your perfect match in every way."

After the way he had made her feel, Donnay felt weak enough to say anything he wanted to hear, but another part of her knew if she did what he asked then he would always consider her putty in his hands. With the strength and willpower that had deserted her earlier, she refused to give in to what he wanted and stubbornly shook her head and said in as firm and absolute voice that she could. "What I just experienced meant nothing. I still say you aren't my type and we are far from being a perfect match."

"Meant nothing?" He gazed down at her, narrowed his eyes for a fraction of a second and then, to her surprise, seconds later smile lines replaced the frown. "Then I will have to work at changing your mind about that, Chardonnay. I hope you're prepared because I love a challenge."

She glared at him. "You can try."

A smile spread from one corner of his lips to the other, and he said, "Don't think for one minute that I won't."

After Spencer opened the rear door to the limousine for Donnay, she hung back. "You aren't riding in the limo to take me home, are you?" she asked with a serious frown on her face.

He met her gaze. "That's my plan."

She narrowed her eyes at him. "Then change it because it's really not necessary."

"I believe that it is. Your mother and grandmother have enough to worry about with your grandfather's illness. They shouldn't have to worry about you, too."

"They won't since they know I can take care of myself," she threw over her shoulder as she slid into the back seat of the car.

"Can you?" he asked, easing into the seat beside her. She scooted over, putting distance between them.

He laughed. "If I wanted to bite, Chardonnay, I would have done so earlier tonight when I had the chance."

His words reminded her of one of the places his teeth had been and the hardened tips of her nipples began throbbing in response to the memory. As much as she wanted to, she couldn't forget the skill of his fingers. She immediately glanced out the window so he wouldn't see her blush. The man had a tendency to say whatever it was that pleased him.

Sensing that his eyes were glued to her, she continued looking out the window as the driver pulled away from his cottage. A part of her was mortified at all the things she had allowed Spencer to do to her tonight, but then another part had been deliciously pleased, although she would never admit such to him.

"Don't forget you only have forty-eight hours to give me your decision, Chardonnay."

That statement made her turn toward him. Then she wished she hadn't. In the dimly lit backseat of the car they were separated from the driver's vision by a deep tinted glass plate. They could see the driver but he couldn't see them. Spencer was lounging casually against the seat in what she assumed he thought was a comfortable position. Personally she thought it was a thoroughly sexy position and to make matters even worse, his gaze was fixed on her.

Tension, as well as desire, began swelling up within and she dragged in a deep breath to force both back down. She knew at that moment that he was someone she should not get involved with, let alone contemplate marrying. Somehow, she would get out of this mess she had gotten both her and her family in. The last thing she wanted was to be under Spencer's control, because whether she admitted it to him or not, the man had proven tonight that he was more than just her type. He had shown just how easy it would be to lose control and give in to him during a weak moment—and she could see herself having plenty of those types of moments with him.

"I need more time than forty-eight hours."

"I'm truly sorry you think that but that's all the time you're getting. You'd have to agree that the plans I have to improve and expand the winery are pretty good ones."

"That isn't the only thing that concerns me," she said, breaking eye contact with him to glance back outside the car's window.

"It should be. Whether you want to admit it or not, I've already proven we're compatible."

She turned back and glared at him. "You've proven no such thing. It was simply a kiss and little fondling that got out of hand."

He started to speak again, stopped and then chuckled before saying, "Think whatever you want. I'm sure the decisions you have to make are rather hard for you, and it's obvious your family depends on you to make the right ones for them. But consider this one thing, Chardonnay. Will you be worse off with me … or without me?"

Conversation between them had stopped several minutes ago and Spencer assumed she was huddled in her corner of the limo angrily sulking. But he should have known that a woman as tough and stubborn as Chardonnay didn't sulk. She had fallen asleep.

He could take that two ways. Either she had gotten bored with him or he had tired her out earlier. And she wanted him to believe she'd merely considered it as a kiss and a little fondling.

He leaned back against the seat as he continued to watch her, thinking she was definitely a sleeping beauty. His stomach knotted when he was assailed by a wave of memories of what had transpired between them earlier that night. Unfamiliar emotions filled him. He wanted more times like that with her, and he wanted the opportunity to take it further without any thoughts of stopping. He wanted her in his bed.

A shudder suddenly raced through him with that obsession. He'd never been so taken with a woman before. He had given her forty-eight hours but in his mind she was already his, and what she didn't know was that he would move heaven or hell to have her. When they had lain together on the sofa, her lithe body had seemed the perfect fit for his and they hadn't even connected intimately yet. Just the thought of being inside her sent previously checked emotions flooding all through him. Everything he was feeling was new to him. New as well as troubling.

He sighed deeply as he continued to watch her sleep, trying to remember the last time he'd done such a thing. With Lynette Marie perhaps? He truly didn't think so. And if he had, it hadn't been with such intensity and concentration like he was doing at this precise moment. Nor with such longing. She evoked a desire and need within him so strong that even now, he was tempted to pull her into his arms and wake her in one rather delicious way. And when the chauffeur turned down the mile-long, scenic lane that would carry them to her home, he thought, why the hell not?

He slid across the seat closer to her, gently caressed the side of her face with his fingertips. "Chardonnay, you're home."

He watched as her eyes slowly opened. She stared at him, seeing how close his face was to hers. "Let's kiss good-night before we get out of the car," he urged in a voice that sounded deep and throaty to his ears.

She continued to stare at him and for a minute he thought she would tell him where he could shove his kiss. Instead he noted the exact moment her breathing became labored. The exact moment her eyes became dilated with a need that mirrored his own.

And when she eased her lips closer to his, the warmth of her breath touched him. He decided at that moment that this kiss would be slow and easy but filled with a fervor he wasn't used to giving or sharing. Deciding he needed to hold her in his arms, hold the body he had possessed and claimed as his earlier, he shifted slightly and pulled her into his lap at the same time he reached out and ran his fingers through her hair before lowering his mouth hungrily to hers.

The moment their mouths touched, connected, locked hard, a hot tide of sensations surged through him. When he felt his insides start to burn, he pulled her closer, and the degree of desire and his ravenous need nearly undid him. She had a taste that was more fulfilling than any meal he could ever eat. Unique, rich and overpowering, it soothed a throbbing ache within him on one hand, and started an agonizing one on the other. He tried dragging his common sense to the forefront, forcing his body to get a grip. But the only grip he wanted was a tighter hold on her. The moment her tongue began dueling with his, pure exhilaration invaded his already fevered body.

He shifted his hips and her right along with them, determined to stroke her bottom. Even through her slacks, cupping her in such a personal way had heat blazing through his veins, groans sounding deep in his chest. The next time they were together this way, he wanted her to wear a dress. It would make it easier when he undressed her. And he intended to undress her and touch her all over. He wanted to make love to every part of her body. Just thinking about all he wanted to do had him wound up tight as a coil.

It was only times like this, when they were seeking mutual satisfaction, that they were on one accord and in tune with each other's wants and needs, willing to give in to their desires. Whether she wanted to accept it or not, she was giving herself to him, had given herself to him earlier that evening. Her actions spoke louder than any words could have, so she might as well make up her mind to become his wife. Besides, he wasn't going to listen to her refusal. He wanted to see that heat in her eyes again, hear her labored breath that signified she was as filled with desire as he was. He wanted to make her wet to his touch, sharing every kind of intimacy with her. He wanted to make her come while embedded deep within her.

Deeply engrossed in the kiss, he hadn't been aware the driver had brought the car to a complete stop until the man thumped on the top of the car. Spencer reluctantly broke off the kiss and pulled back and gazed down at her. There was nothing she could say. No denials, no accusations, no crying foul play. Not this time.

She had wanted the kiss, had enjoyed it as much as he had and they both knew it. Besides, over the next forty-eight hours they both had a lot to think about. He needed to understand why he was swamped by emotions he hadn't known he had. How this young, wisp of a woman could overwhelm him the way she had, so quickly and deeply.

"Forty-eight hours," he whispered softly against her moist lips.

Instead of the flaming retort he expected, she nodded and then pulled herself out of his arms, straightening her clothes. He watched her draw in a huge breath before glancing over at him. She exhaled slowly and said, "Are you sure you want me as a wife? I really don't think you know what you're asking for."

He thought about all the satisfaction he'd gotten from what they'd shared back at his place and the limo ride home, all the satisfaction and fulfillment a future with her would bring, and countered by saying, "Yes, I want you as my wife, and I know exactly what I'm asking for."

Seven

Forty-eight hours.

She had only ten of those left and she'd yet to make a decision.

Donnay sighed as she stepped out of the shower and grabbed a towel to dry her body. She reassessed the predicament that she and her family were now facing, and although she didn't want to admit it, marriage to Spencer was the only solution, especially after talking to her grandfather's doctor yesterday. His condition was improving; however, sooner or later he would need the surgery, and the insurance company would deny paying for it since it was considered experimental treatment. That meant even if she opted for the loan, they would run the risk of not being able to keep up the mortgage payments.

She then thought, as she finished dressing for the day, about the pros and cons of marrying Spencer.

She would have to endure a loveless marriage, which was the main thing she couldn't get past just yet. She would have to willingly subject herself to spending the rest of her life with a man who didn't love her and would never love her. Given his attitude toward love, she wondered about the woman responsible for breaking his heart.

On the flip side, if she agreed to marry him, her family's financial worries would be over. And the added plus was that he had agreed to take the winery to the next level. Staying a regional mom-and-pop operation had served its usefulness. In order to compete in a broader market and bring in a higher profit, changes needed to be made, and they were changes that could only come about with Spencer's financial support.

She sighed deeply, feeling like the sacrificial lamb. If she were to tell her mother and grandparents about Spencer's outlandish proposal they would be outraged. On the other hand, if she were to waltz in and tell them she had fallen in love with him and planned to marry him, they would become suspicious anyway, since she had made it pretty clear that she detested the man.

The good thing was that she hadn't heard from Spencer since that night he had brought her home in the limo. She considered his absence a blessing. The last thing she needed was for him to further mess with her already muddled mind. With his hands she had been on the brink of her first real orgasm and just thinking about it had hot streaks of sensations rushing through all parts of her. One thing their marriage wouldn't lack was passion. He had more in his mouth and fingers than most men had in their entire body. He wanted kids and she didn't doubt he would have her pregnant within the first year. But then she had longed for kids, and a husband who would love her. Getting one out of two wasn't so bad, she told herself.

Her mind then went back to the passion. Spencer had touched her in ways she had never before been touched, making her feel things she'd never before felt. What happened to her whenever she was around him? Why was it so easy for him to entice her to indulge in things that she really didn't want to do? And why was the thought of being married to him turning her on instead of turning her off?

She knew one thing that was for certain, he was wiggling his way into her family's affections. According to her grandmother and mother, he had visited with her grandfather at the hospital yesterday, and of course everyone thought it had been extremely kind of him to do so.

She glanced around when she heard the knock at the door. "Yes?"

"I have a delivery for you, Ms. Russell."

Donnay felt relieved it was Janice, their housekeeper, and not her mother or grandmother. No doubt they would have questions about the loan. It had been three days since she'd told them they had been approved and she had yet to act on it and they had to be wondering why. As far as they were concerned the loan was the only hope for the winery's survival.

"Come on in, Janice."

Janice walked in carrying a huge vase of red roses that was almost larger than she was. In her late fifties, she was a tiny thing, barely five feet, weighing a little over a hundred pounds. She and her family had worked in one capacity or another at Russell Vineyards for years.

"What on earth," Donnay exclaimed, immediately crossing the room to relieve Janice of the megasize delivery.

The older woman smiled. "They just arrived for you. Aren't they gorgeous?"

Donnay smiled. Yes, they were, and it wasn't hard to figure out who had sent them. "Yes, they are nice," she said, pulling off the card and then making space for the vase on the table that faced the window.

"Well, I need to get back downstairs and prepare Ms. Ruth's and Ms. Catherine's breakfast."

As soon as the door closed behind Janice, Donnay pulled open the card that simply read: *Thinking of you. Spencer.*

Donnay rolled her eyes. In other words, he was sending her a reminder that her time was running out and he expected her decision in the time frame he had given. But when she glanced over at the roses, she had to admit he'd given her a very beautiful reminder.

She remembered the words Spencer had spoken two nights ago, and he was right. She had to decide, in ten hours or less, if she would be worse off with him in her life than she would be without him in it.

Spencer pulled his BlackBerry out of his jacket to check stock market results after noticing Daniel Russell had drifted off to sleep. He could vividly recall sitting at his own grandfather's hospital bedside years ago.

Scott Westmoreland's death from lung cancer had been hard on the Westmorelands since he had been the rock of the family. All of his grandsons, and at the time the one lone granddaughter, Delaney, had learned something from him that would carry them through life to face the many challenges and hardships.

As he placed the BlackBerry back in his jacket, he glanced back over at Chardonnay's grandfather. Yesterday, the two had talked and Daniel had asked if he would return today to shave him and he had. Also yesterday, the man had been a lot more talkative. He had shared with him all his hopes and dreams for the winery and had apologetically told Spencer that he regretted they wouldn't be selling the vineyard to him after all, but that they felt strongly that it should remain in the Russell family. His words had let Spencer know Chardonnay had yet to tell her family about his offer. He didn't know if that was a good sign or a bad one. But a part of him was confident she would end up doing the right thing—which would be to marry him.

Suddenly he became aware that someone was watching him. He glanced up and felt a tantalizing throb in his gut when he saw it was Chardonnay. At that very instant it seemed that he couldn't breathe. She was standing in the doorway to the hospital room staring at him. Her eyes weren't glaring or shooting daggers at him. They were just staring. He was certain she was wondering why he was there, and before she could ask, he stood and beckoned her to follow him into the hall so they could speak privately and not disturb her grandfather.

"I dropped by this morning to shave him," Spencer said as soon as they had stepped into the hall.

She nodded. "I know. Mom told me that he asked you to do it yesterday. Any one of us could have done it for him but I guess it's a man's thing." She then smiled sheepishly and said, "Or it could be that the last time we shaved him we left him with quite a few cuts and nicks."

"Ouch." His response made her laugh and Spencer found himself relaxing somewhat…as well as taking the time to notice her outfit. She was wearing a pair of jeans and a light-blue pullover sweater. Both looked good on her and the light-blue brought out the color of her eyes in a pretty way.

"Thanks for the flowers. They're beautiful," she said.

"You're welcome."

When a moment passed and they didn't say anything, she said, "We need to talk, Spencer. I've made my decision but I don't want to go into it here."

He met her gaze. "Okay. Let's have dinner tonight."

"All right, but not at your place again."

He started to argue, to tell her she was in no position to make decisions, but then thought better of it. Dinner tonight would be about decisions—hers—and he wanted to know which ones she had made no matter where they dined.

"And I prefer meeting you someplace. Don't waste your time sending a car for me because I won't get in it," she added curtly.

He nodded. "Okay, I won't be sending a car for you. I'm coming to pick you up myself and I do expect you to get in."

He saw her stiffen, her jaw set tight. "I'll be there to pick you up at five," he said.

She glanced down at the floor where she was tapping her foot. Probably counting to ten to hold back her anger, he thought. She had a tendency to dislike him giving her orders. "Are we on this evening for dinner at five, Chardonnay?" he asked, deciding to make sure they were on the same page.

She glanced back up at him. Her gaze was made of stone. "Do I have a choice?"

"No."

He said it quickly and unerringly.

"I have a request to make of you," she said, and from the look in her eyes he knew he wouldn't like it.

"What?"

"Promise me that you'll keep your hands and lips to yourself tonight."

He couldn't help but smile at that one. "Does that mean I can't kiss you…or touch you anywhere I want?" he asked as calmly as he could.

"Yes, that's exactly what it means."

He shrugged broad shoulders. "In that case I won't make such a promise because I plan to kiss you, Chardonnay. I like kissing you, and as long as you kiss me back, letting me know you're enjoying the kiss as much as I am, I see no reason to stop. And need I remind you that you initiated the last kiss we shared. I might have had my mouth in the right place at the right time, but it was you who made the first move."

He hated reminding her of that, but she needed to hear it. She needed to know that he was fully aware each and every time she participated in their kiss. "But as far as touching you like I did before, unless you give me a reason to think you want me to touch you there, I won't, since I've accomplished what I intended to do."

She frowned. "Which was?"

"Claim it as mine." Before she could open her mouth to deny his words, he said. "When your grandfather wakes, let him know I'll be stopping by again tomorrow."

"Why?" she asked when he was about to turn and leave.

He smiled. "Mainly because I like him. He reminds me a lot of my own grandfather and I was close to him. All his grandchildren were. He left a huge void in our lives when he died. He was a good man, and I believe your grandfather is a good man as well."

Deciding not to say anything else, he walked off toward the bank of elevators.

"Did your grandfather wake up and ask about me?"

Donnay turned from gazing out the car window to find Spencer looking over at her when he'd stopped at a traffic light. Just like he'd said, he had arrived exactly at five. She had been ready.

"Yes, and he seemed pleased that you would be returning tomorrow," she said, not liking it but being totally honest. She could tell her grandfather liked Spencer. So did her mother and grandmother. "You never said where we're going," she decided to say when the car began moving again.

"Into San Francisco. There's a nice restaurant I want to take you to. I think you're going to like it."

She was sure she would since it seemed that Spencer Westmoreland didn't do anything half-measure.

"Tell me about this surgery the doctor wants your grandfather to have."

She glanced over at him. "Who told you about it?" she asked, annoyed. It was family business and he wasn't family.

"Your mother and grandmother. They seemed worried that it wouldn't be covered by the insurance."

She wished her family hadn't taken Spencer into their confidence. But they didn't know how he could use such information to his benefit. However, since they had done so, she figured she might as well level with him. "There's a good chance it won't be since it's considered experimental."

"And if they don't, what's your next option?"

She sighed deeply. Did he look at all solutions by way of options? "If the insurance company denies payment then we'll pay for it out of our pockets. Either way, if Gramps needs that surgery then he's going to have it."

She knew Spencer was probably taking this all in and in doing so figured she had only one option open to her. The one he wanted her to take. He must be feeling pretty good knowing he had her family stuck between a rock and a hard place.

"You're right," he said, breaking into her thoughts. "Either way if your grandfather needs that surgery then he's going to get it. I'll take care of the cost, no matter what option you've decided to take."

Donnay snatched her head around, thinking she had definitely not heard him correctly. He'd come to another traffic light and was looking at her. "Why would you do that?" she asked, barely getting the words out and staring at him wide-eyed.

"Would you believe because I'm a nice guy?" he asked.

"No. I think that you can be a nice guy but that usually you aren't."

He chuckled. "My family would be the first to disagree with you. The personal side of me is nice all the time, but oftentimes, I have to take on another persona when I'm negotiating business. It comes with the territory. In that arena, nice guys finish last, and I like being first."

She believed him. "I don't want you to think the Russells are a charity case that need your handout, Spencer."

"I appreciate you telling me that, Chardonnay," he said, and she easily picked up the edge in his voice. "But the truth remains, charity case or not, your family needs my financial assistance and I'm willing to give it either way. Do you have a problem with that?"

Saying she did would, in essence, be the same as biting off her nose to spite her face, and she was too smart to do that. There was such a thing as family pride, but then there was also such a thing as knowing when to exercise good common sense. "No, I don't have a problem with it. Thank you for making the offer."

"You're welcome. And now it seems that we've arrived at our destination."

A frown darkened Spencer's brow as he watched Chardonnay finish the last of her dessert. What he'd told her in the car was true in most circumstances, but he was finding himself being a rather nice guy in his business dealings with her. Case in point, he hadn't immediately asked for her decision the moment the two of them had sat down to dinner. Nor had he inquired as to what it was over dinner. Instead he had engaged her in conversation about other things, things he normally didn't give a damn about, like who was messing around with whom in Hollywood or which rapper had offended Bill O'Reilly or vice versa.

Now he couldn't put off asking any longer, nor did he intend to. "So what have you decided, Chardonnay?"

He watched as she lifted her head and her gray eyes stared at him. She placed her fork down then took a napkin and wiped her lips. They were lips he had thought about kissing all evening. Suddenly the room seemed to get silent as he tuned everything out to concentrate on one thing. Her decision.

She continued to look at him directly and he knew whatever she'd decided that he hadn't made things easy for her. That had been deliberate on his part. But now, if her decision went the way he wanted, she wouldn't have to think of anything hard again. He would guarantee it... Almost. There was still that question regarding her degree of loyalty. That was important to him and it was something he had to be certain that he had from her, no matter what.

"I've decided to marry you, Spencer."

Her statement seared through him, made his heart squeeze tight and had blood pulsing rapidly through his veins. She bowed her head to resume eating and a frown gathered between his brows. Had she really meant it? His jaw tightened at the thought that she was playing with him.

"Chardonnay?"

"Yes?" She lifted her head again and for a long moment his eyes stared into hers. A deep desire to have her slowly replaced any irritating thought he'd had. She had been serious. She would marry him. For better or for worse. And she was accepting her fate of a loveless marriage. He gave a mental shrug, refusing to feel guilty. It was her decision.

"We need to make plans. I want the wedding to take place before Christmas."

Her eyes widened. "That's impossible. Christmas is less than three weeks from now."

"I know. We had a Christmas wedding in the family last year when my cousin Chase married. In fact it was on Christmas Day. Everyone had to make arrangements to be away from their homes during the holidays to attend. At this late date some people may have already made other plans this year. I prefer having a private ceremony before Christmas, here in the valley with just our families."

She narrowed her eyes at him. "What's the rush?"

"I'm surprised you would ask me that, Chardonnay." He knew she could read between the lines quite clearly and she proved it when her cheeks darkened.

"I guess you wouldn't entertain the thought of us waiting to get to know each other a lot better before engaging in something so intimate," she said softly.

"No, I wouldn't," he said quickly, deciding to once again make his position clear. "I want you, Chardonnay. I've never hidden that fact. And I want babies. Marrying you will give me all the things I want and you will benefit from the marriage as well."

A frown formed on her face. "And what will you tell your family about us? What am I supposed to tell mine?"

He picked up his wineglass to take a sip. "We'll tell them we met and fell in love immediately. It will be a lie of course, but considering …"

She raised a brow. "And they're supposed to believe it? Just like that?" she asked, snapping her fingers.

He leaned forward. "Yes, just like that," he said, snapping his own fingers. He chuckled. "My mother won't have a problem believing it since she's a true romantic."

He then straightened in his chair and said, "I'm flying out to L.A. for a few days to attend several prescheduled business meetings. When I get back I plan to move into your home, so make room."

"What?" She looked incredulous.

"Now that you've given me your decision—one I will trust you to keep—work will begin on the winery immediately after I get back and I need to be around for that. If there's not room for me at the main house, I'll settle with living in one of the guest cottages. I'll remain there until we marry."

From her expression he could tell he was moving too fast for her, but he had no intentions of slowing down.

Donnay stood outside her mother's bedroom door, trying to get a grip on her nerves. She had exchanged very few words with Spencer during the drive back home from the restaurant. Instead they preferred the silence since there had been very little left to be said.

Now she was to convince her family that she had miraculously fallen in love with him. Her grandparents might fall for that story but her mother would see through it. Taking in a deep breath, Donnay knocked on the door.

"Come in."

Donnay opened the door, stepped into the room and paused. Her mother was dressed to go out and she looked absolutely stunning. She couldn't recall the last time her mother wore something out other than slacks and a blouse. Tonight she was wearing a dress Donnay had never seen before. The soft tobacco-brown fabric slithered down her mother's curves.

"You're going out, Mom?" Donnay asked, although the answer was obvious.

Her mother gave her an easy smile. "Yes. How do I look?"

"Beautiful."

"That's good. That friend I told you about who's passing through, we're meeting for dinner tonight."

Donnay continued to look at her mom. "In that case I think you look too beautiful to be going out with an old girlfriend. You should be going on a date with a man."

Her mother chuckled. "Haven't we had this discussion before?"

"Yes, several times," Donnay agreed, leaning against the closed door.

"And what have I always told you?" her mother asked.

She'd always told her that she could never love another man the way she'd loved her father and that she was content and didn't need another man in her life, a man she could never love. Donnay wondered if that was the same for Spencer. Was there a woman out there whom he loved and that was the reason he could not love another?

"You're worried about something, Donnay," her mother said, breaking into her thoughts. "Come. Let's sit and talk." Her mother sat down on the bed.

With a deep sigh, Donnay crossed the room to take a seat beside her mother.

"Okay, tell me what's bothering you."

Donnay let out a breath, not sure how she was going to say it. Then she decided to just get it out. She turned toward her mother. "Mom, it's about Spencer Westmoreland."

Ruth raised a brow. "What about Mr. Westmoreland? Did you know he came back to visit your grandfather today?"

"Yes, I know."

"I think your grandfather likes him."

"I can believe that."

Ruth studied her daughter. "So what's bothering you about Mr. Westmoreland?"

Donnay felt her stomach tighten into knots. "He's asked me to marry him, Mom, and he wants to have a private ceremony here in the valley before Christmas."

Ruth looked stunned. "You're kidding aren't you, sweetheart?"

Donnay shook her head. "No, Mom, I'm not kidding and it's the only way."

Ruth frowned. "The only way for what?"

Donnay took the next twenty minutes to tell her mother everything, including the details of the loan as well as Spencer's proposal.

Her mother didn't say anything for a moment then said in a relatively calm voice, "You must have misunderstood Mr. Westmoreland."

Donnay rolled her eyes. Spencer had her mother and grandparents convinced that he was Mr. Nice Guy. "Trust me, Mom, I understood Spencer perfectly."

Ruth shook her head. "If what you say is true, Donnay, then how can you even think your grandparents and I would let you go ahead with such a marriage? You mean more to us than the winery."

Instinctively Donnay reached out and took her mother's hand in hers. "I know, Mom, but it's something I must do."

Ruth studied her daughter. "And could it be something that you *want* to do as well?"

Donnay couldn't believe that her mother would ask such a thing. "Of course not. You of all people know how I feel about that man."

Ruth patted her daughter's hand a few times before asking, "Did I ever tell you that I disliked your father at first, too?"

Donnay looked back at her mother, surprised. "No, you never mentioned that. I assumed, considering how much you loved him, that it was love at first sight."

Ruth chuckled. "Far from it. I saw him as a threat."

Donnay lifted her brow. "A threat? To what?"

"To my relationship with Dad. Dad hired him on and the two of them quickly became close. I saw Chad as the son Dad never had, and I began thinking that Dad would regret I was born a girl and not a boy who would carry on the Russell name."

Donnay thought about what her mother had said for a moment then asked, "Did my father know how you felt?"

"Yes, I wasn't the easiest person to get along with and at times I deliberately made things hard for him. At least I tried to. But he saw through it all. And for some reason he understood."

Her mother got quiet and Donnay knew she was remembering those times, and recapturing those moments. It had to be hard for her mother. Donnay wished there was a way she could convince her to leave the valley for a while to find the man she loved and had allowed to walk out of her life. There had been times while in college when Donnay had been tempted to look up Chad Timberlain, get to meet the father she never knew and who didn't know she existed. But she never did.

For all she knew, and what her mother suspected, he

was now married with other children. Children who were her half siblings. She never got the courage to find him because she hadn't ever wanted to be the one to verify her mother's assumptions that the man she loved and had let get away had another life that included a wife and children.

"Mom, I appreciate you sharing that with me about you and Dad, but the situation with me and Spencer is totally different. I appreciate what he did for Gramps, but he's not the man you and Grammy think that he is."

Her mother touched her arm. "And considering everything, I have a feeling he's not the man you think that he is, either, Donnay."

Eight

An aura of intense longing swept over Spencer the moment he rounded the corner of the building where he was told he would find Chardonnay doing a wine tasting. It had been almost a week since he'd seen her and he'd been stunned as to just how much he'd missed her, to the point that once his plane had landed in San Francisco, he had driven straight to the Russell Vineyard.

He followed the sound of voices and stepped into the crowded tasting room. Chardonnay was to taste the first wine to be bottled and packaged from this season's pruned crop. If the wine passed her inspection, it would continue to age.

Shivers of awareness passed through him when he saw her. She was standing on a platform facing the crowd—a Russell who was about to place verdict on a Russell wine. She stood before a table that held four glasses filled with wine. Sun shining through the huge windows slanted glints of gold on her head, adding highlights to her hair. Emotion gripped his gut at the sight of her. She was the most strikingly beautiful woman he knew, the woman who would become his wife and the mother of his children. She had been on his mind constantly since he'd left the valley, but no memory could compare with the woman in the flesh.

He watched as she rotated the glass a few times on the table. According to what he knew about wine tasting, she was swirling the wine around in the glass to mix it with air. The motion would cause the aromatic compound in the wine to vaporize and get that unique smell.

Moments later she picked up the glass and brought it to her face, sticking her nose into the airspace of the glass where the aromas were captured. Tempting visions, erotic in nature, filled his mind and fueled his imagination. While she was concentrating on the wine's scent, he was remembering hers, the one he considered sharply seductive, the one that could send sensations racing through him the moment it filled his nostrils.

Trying to get a grip, he watched as her eyes closed before she took a sip. He remembered another time he had watched her close her eyes like that. That night she had been at his place. The same night he had decided that no matter what it took, he had to make Chardonnay Russell his.

She opened her eyes and the smile that touched her lips was priceless. He knew the wine she had just tasted had successfully passed her inspection. Of course it would go through other tasters, but everyone knew her opinion counted most. Nodding her approval, she moved on to the next glass.

He leaned back against a solid wall. He had a clear view of her but doubted she had seen him yet, which was just fine. She would know his presence in all things, especially her life, soon enough.

His trip to Los Angles had been very productive. He had met with Steve Carr, the man whose construction company would be responsible for the expansions he wanted made to the winery. Work would begin rather quickly and he was getting excited about it and couldn't wait to tell Chardonnay so she could share his excitement.

When he heard everyone around him clapping, his concentration went back to Chardonnay. She had tasted all four glasses and evidently had approved all of them. Then, as her gaze spanned the crowd, she saw him. The moment their eyes connected, even if only for a brief second, he felt it as well as saw it. He saw the darkening of her eyes at the same moment he felt deep need pass through him.

She broke eye contact to speak with the people who had begun gathering around her. After she thanked them for upholding the Russell tradition in producing superb wine, she excused herself from the group and began walking his way. He hadn't moved an inch and his gaze flicked across her from head to toe as she made her way toward him.

He was mesmerized, utterly captivated. And not for the first time he was asking himself how one woman could snag a man's emotions so thoroughly and completely.

"You're back," she said in a tone of voice that didn't give away whether she was delighted or disappointed.

"Yes, I'm back. Have you set a date for the wedding?" he decided to ask, thinking there was no reason not to.

She gave a resigned shrug of her shoulders and her voice was very cool when she said, "Did I have a choice?"

If she expected a softening of his heart, she wasn't getting it today. "That depends on what you want and what's important to you," he replied in a voice that was painstakingly clear. "And I thought we'd gotten beyond all of that, Chardonnay. No need to whine about it now."

She narrowed her gaze. "Is that what you think I'm doing?"

"Sounds like it. What I was really hoping for was a nice welcome-home kiss."

"Sorry to disappoint you," she said sarcastically.

She had disappointed him but not surprised him. He smiled, thinking he would make doubly sure she made up for it later. However, he definitely wouldn't tell her that. Instead he decided to change the subject. "I spoke with your grandfather yesterday. He sounds good."

She smiled and he could tell it was genuine and sincere. "Yes, we're all pleased with his progress. If it continues he'll be able to come home at the end of the week. The doctor wants to give him time to build up his strength before planning the next phase of his treatment."

"The surgery?"

"Yes. They want to schedule it sometime after the holidays, providing his health continues to improve. I'm going to visit with him later. Would you like to come with me?"

He was surprised by the invitation and had no intentions of turning it down. "Yes, I'd like that, but first

I need to make arrangements to have my things moved here from the Chablis."

He watched her mouth tighten. "You're still planning on living here?"

"Yes, nothing has changed," he said in an even tone. "All my plans are still the same. The ones I have for the winery as well as the ones I have for us. And speaking of which, your mother said you would be the one to show me to the guest villa."

"Yes, I guess I am," she said, her voice trailing off as she turned around and noticed everyone had begun to leave.

"Yes, sweetheart, you definitely are," he said softly.

Donnay turned back to Spencer, trying not to let the throaty tone of his voice take over her senses and make her forget how he had succeeded in turning her entire life upside down. And then there was the term of endearment he'd just used. *Sweetheart*. It had a nice ring to it, but was actually meaningless in their situation.

The shutting of the door claimed her attention and she was grateful for the distraction until she saw that everyone had gone and she and Spencer were left alone. Definitely not a good thing. Especially when simply standing close to him was making all sorts of wanton thoughts flow through her head. Those boundaries she had set the last time they'd been together were fading away and she couldn't let that happen.

"If you're ready, I can walk you over to the guest villa. It's not far from here," she heard herself saying, as she took a step back, away from him.

In a surprised move, one she hadn't been prepared for,

he reached out, snagged her arm and pulled her back closer. "Not yet. There's something I need to do first."

His touch had every nerve in her body tingling and as usual she was immediately drawn to him. From the look in his eyes she knew he wanted to kiss her, was going to kiss her, and as much as she didn't want to, she was felt the anticipation of his kiss all the way down to the bone. She refused to play coy. She wanted this.

"Do you know how many nights I lay awake thinking about you?" he whispered, leaning closer to let his mouth brush her cheek. She could feel the warmth of his breath on the underside of her ear. Not waiting for her response, he answered his own question by saying in a husky voice, "Way too many nights."

And then unerringly, his mouth found hers, locked on to it, claimed it and successfully obliterated any and all coherent thoughts from her mind. Instead she concentrated on only one thing—his tongue and the way it was stroking hers, tangling with it in a deeply intimate way, sending sensuous chills up her spine, making goose bumps form on her arms and leaving no doubt in her mind that he had succeeded in touching something deep inside of her once again. He moved her in a way no other man could and she doubted ever would. A part of her knew she should reclaim her senses, put on the brakes. But she couldn't, nor did she want to. The way he was kissing her, so deep, sensual and intimate, he was making it plainly difficult, absolutely impossible, not to respond in kind. So she did.

She knew the exact moment her arms voluntarily reached around his neck to hold his mouth to hers, as well as when she felt his warm, hard fingers entwine in her hair. She also felt the heat of his body pressed intimately to hers, every hard plane and indentation, and she sank helplessly deeper into his strength, while he sank deeper into her mouth. His kiss was filling her with a physical yearning she only encountered with him.

When their lips finally parted, he pulled her closer into his arms, holding her, and they remained that way, silent for the moment.

Knowing she couldn't afford to give in to any sort of weakness or throw away good common sense, she pulled out of his arms. "I think we need to make some ground rules," she said in a shaky breath.

"I don't," was his response, as he brushed a stray curl back from her face. "Every time I kiss you that way, I want to proceed and strip you naked."

Like he'd come close to doing that other night, she thought. "I'd rather keep my clothes on around you. I think it's safer."

"Safer but not as satisfying. I think you should stop trying to fight me, Chardonnay, and give in to your wants and desires."

She shook her head. "I can't."

He held her gaze. "Yes, you can and eventually you will. We are perfect for each other."

She inhaled deeply as her mind absorbed his words. He might think the two of them were perfect but she did not. She refused to become too enthralled with any man again, let him take over her mind and thoughts. Besides that, Spencer was a man who could wiggle his way into a woman's heart if she wasn't careful. He would have her falling in love with him even though she knew he would never love her back.

"I would have to disagree with that," she said with conviction. "Now I suggest that I show you to the guest villa."

She hoped they were back to square one. No matter how much she might respond to his kiss and intimate caresses, she had to prove that nothing had changed. She still considered him a threat to her happiness.

As they walked along the path, Donnay was surprised at how relaxed she suddenly felt in Spencer's presence. It was as if the torrid kiss they'd shared moments ago had been what she needed to ease the tension.

"How many guest houses do you have?" Spencer asked, breaking into the silence surrounding them. They were strolling a path very familiar to her, one she had always enjoyed as a child because the area surrounding it was always manicured, while the land beyond was overgrown with blackberry, raspberry and tomato vines.

"We have four guest villas, and a gardener's cottage that's located at the edge of the vineyard," she said, remembering the day she had planted her very first grapevine nearby. Her grandfather had given her the space to grow her own to keep her from picking and eating the ones to be used for the wines.

"The guest villa you'll be staying in is actually where I was going to live when I returned from college. I never moved in since I preferred staying at the big house with my mother and grandparents. I felt it would be lonely living there and too far away from things."

"But you will be living there with me, once we're married."

She glanced over at him. He hadn't asked a question but had made a statement he expected her to obey. A part of her wanted to rebel but she knew there was no use. In the end he would get what he wanted. "Yes, I'll be living there with you."

He smiled, seemingly satisfied with her acceptance of her fate. "Will you help me move in today?" he then asked.

Considering they seemed to be drawn together like magnets whenever they were alone, she didn't think that was a good idea. "There are some things I need to do before visiting Gramps at the hospital."

He nodded. "I understand and that's fine. But I'm counting on you to help me later since I'm sure I'll still have a few things that will need unpacking when we get back from the hospital."

She knew he was letting her know that he wouldn't allow her to put distance between them. Whether she liked it or not, they would be spending time together later tonight. "We had the phone service and electricity turned on a few days ago so you're all set," she said.

"Okay."

When they didn't say anything for several moments, he broke the silence by asking, "So you said you'd decided on a date?"

"Yes, I thought two weeks from this Saturday would do it. What do you think?"

He chuckled. "I think it's time to give my family a call and tell them about you. Of course they would want to attend the wedding ceremony. Wild horses won't be able to keep Mom away." He tilted his head and looked at her. "I see you've already told yours since your grandmother and mother congratulated me and welcomed me to the family when I arrived today."

She shrugged. "I saw no reason not to go ahead and

tell them. I basically told my mother the truth regarding our relationship. However, I led Grammy to believe we miraculously fell in love."

"And your grandfather?"

She stopped walking and gazed up at him. "I haven't told him anything yet, and Mom and Grammy promised they wouldn't, either. I thought it was best to wait until you returned so we could tell him together."

Spencer nodded. "And how do you think he'll take the news?"

Donnay couldn't help the wry smile that touched her lips. "Oh, he'll handle it quite nicely since your plans fall so neatly in with his. He's been after me for some time about finding a man, settling down and giving him great-grandkids. So in essence, you'll be giving him something he truly wants."

"And it's something I truly want as well," he said, smiling over at her. "And I'm more than happy to oblige."

They began walking again and she was glad moments later when they came to the private path that led to the guest villa where he would be staying. As soon as she got him there she planned to hightail it to the nearest shower to cool off. The man had a way of heating her body with a touch or a mere look. Resisting him was becoming a challenge.

"This path leads to the villa, the one you'll be using," she said, turning to walk a few steps ahead of him down the trail. "It's surrounded by a wrought-iron fence and is secluded enough to assure complete privacy. It's like your own little world inside a bigger universe."

He smiled. "It reminds me of a French château and I like it already," he said when he reached the gate and he saw the huge two-story structure. From his expression she could tell it was more than he had expected. "Who was this place built for?" he asked when she opened the gate for them to enter.

"No one in particular. The other villas are relatively small compared to this one and Gramps wanted to construct one that was larger and roomier. Like I said earlier, I think it was meant for me, although he would never admit he would do anything to persuade me to stay if I ever decided to leave. He felt pretty bad about what happened between my mother and father."

Spencer lifted a brow. "What happened between your parents?"

Donnay glanced over at him as they strolled up the walkway toward the front door. "They met when my father took a summer job here. He was in the army and was working at the winery while waiting to be deployed. He met and fell in love with my mother and she fell in love with him, too. He tried convincing her to marry him and travel the world with him since he planned on making the military a career. Although she loved him, she turned down his marriage proposal and sent him away because she didn't want to leave my grandparents alone. She felt her place was here with them at the vineyard. It was only after he left that she discovered she was pregnant with me."

Spencer paused, his hand on the doorknob. "So he never knew about you?"

"No. She tried writing him but the letter came back. Evidently he moved around a lot in the military."

"And you never tried finding him?"

She shook her head. "No. It's not that I never wanted to know Chad Timberlain—it's just that I knew developing a relationship with him would be a constant reminder to my mother of the love she gave away. That would be painful for her, especially if he had eventually married someone else over the years. My grandfather has always felt he and Grammy were unintentionally responsible for Mom turning her back on her true love, although they tried convincing her they would be fine here and that she should follow her heart."

When he opened the door she took a step back. "You don't really need me to give you a tour of the place so I'll leave you alone now."

He leaned in the open doorway, his stance nearly overpowering. "What time do you want to leave for the hospital?"

"Anytime after five will be okay. Grammy is spending the night with Gramps tonight. We prefer that she didn't because she'll be sleeping on a cot they bring into the hospital room, which won't be all that comfortable. However, no matter what Mom and I say she's determined to do so. After fifty years of marriage, I think she misses him."

He nodded. "I understand. Although my parents haven't been married quite that long, they have a strong marriage as well."

"Do they?"

"Yes. Like I told you, strong and long-lasting marriages run in the Westmoreland family."

Yes, he had told her that. "Well, I'll see you later," she said backing up to leave. If you'd like, you're welcome at lunch. Grammy usually has it on the table around one. If you want to get back to the main house just follow the path and you won't get lost."

"All right and thanks for the invitation. I might take you up on it."

"You're welcome," she said, forcing a cheerful smile before turning and quickly walking away.

"I appreciate you offering to help," Spencer said, ignoring Chardonnay's raised brow as he opened the door to the villa later that night. He knew she was thinking she hadn't offered. He really hadn't given her a choice in the matter.

She hesitated before stepping over the threshold and he strolled in behind her, closing and locking the door. He watched her glance around for a few minutes, and then she turned to him with a bemused expression. "I expected to see boxes all over the place."

He smiled in a perfectly calm way. "Did you?"

"Yes. You said you needed my help putting things away."

"I do. But everything didn't arrive today, so I have time."

The suspicion he saw in her eyes then became more pronounced. "In that case why am I here?" she asked, placing her hands on her hips "Why did you lead me to believe that you needed me tonight?"

She would have to ask, he thought as he leaned against the closed door and stared at her. And since she had, he would be completely honest when he gave her an answer. "Because I *do* need you tonight."

Donnay inhaled sharply. The tone of his voice, the intent of his words both were a soft caress across her skin. Their gazes held and she felt it, unquestionably.

His eyes were so dark she actually felt their intensity, could see the desire lining their depths. An instant passed, and then another and she felt herself getting breathless beneath the depth of their attraction for each other. Regardless of wanting to deny it, she couldn't.

She opened her lips to say whatever he needed tonight was his problem and not hers, but closed them when shivers raced up her spine. He was doing that to her and hadn't even touched her, hadn't even moved away from the door. His concentrated stare was making crazy things happen to her.

Sensations began gripping her and she felt the tips of her breasts grow hard as she remembered his mouth, tongue and teeth on them. She also remembered the place his fingers had been and felt a sudden ferocious ache right between her legs. She shook her head, trying to clear her mind of such memories and found it was no use. She then concluded that what she had deemed as *his* problem was now *her* problem as well.

She watched as he came toward her and she had the mind to take a step back and couldn't. Every fiber in her being was attuned to him, attracted to him, aroused by him. She couldn't resist him any longer. Nor did she want to.

"I want you and I need you, Chardonnay," he whispered huskily when he came to a stop in front of her.

She tilted her head back and looked at him, felt the heat coming from his gaze. And when he reached out and slipped his hands around her waist, bringing her body against the solid hardness of him, she inhaled when she felt his rock-hard erection press against the juncture of her thighs. Even the denim of her skirt couldn't downplay just how firm he was.

For moments he held her close against him, as if he needed the contact as much as she did. It then became crystal clear that her life and her future were going to be tied to him. He said he wanted a long-term marriage and a bunch of kids and she believed him; so why not accept how things were destined to be for her and move on? Why continue to fight what she couldn't change? Her grandfather was happy about their pending marriage, so was her grandmother. However, she could tell her mother was more worried than elated.

"Chardonnay?"

She tilted up her head to stare into his face. "Yes?" He was a strikingly handsome man. The thought of having a son or daughter who shared his features pulled on her heartstrings.

"I've told you what I want and need. Now it's your turn. Tell me what I can do for you tonight. If you say there's nothing you want or need from me then I will accept that and walk you back home. But if you have desires, I will not let you leave here unsatisfied."

Donnay swallowed because that's what she was afraid of. Spencer had unraveled her emotions in a way that Robert never had. What she should do was tell him good night and leave. Instead she found herself asking in a soft, curious voice, after remembering her intimate times with Robert, "What makes you think you can?"

He raised a dark brow. "Can what?"

"Satisfy me."

She watched as a slow, confident smile touched both corners of his lips. "Why would you think I can't?"

Since they would be getting married soon and he was determined that they would share a bed, she decided to be honest with him. She might be one of those women a man couldn't completely satisfy. "Robert didn't."

His brow arched higher. "The professor?"

"Yes, the one and only guy I've slept with."

"I can't imagine any man making love to you and not making you feel like an explosion hit and that every part of you has been shot to the stars and beyond."

Donnay's couldn't imagine anyone making her feel that way. "And how will you accomplish that?"

The look in his eyes indicated that he couldn't believe she really had to ask. But he answered anyway. "First, I'll undress you, kissing every part of you that I expose, lingering on some areas a lot longer than others. Next I'll take you into the bedroom and engage in foreplay of the most intense kind. So intense that I'll have you begging."

She shook her head. He'd made that claim before and she recalled how close she'd come to doing just that the night when he'd invited her to his place at the Chablis. "Is that what you think, that you'll make me beg?"

"No, sweetheart, that's what I know. In addition to long marriages, there's something else Westmorelands are known for."

She was almost afraid to ask but did so anyway. "And what's that?"

"Satisfying their mates. We are extremely physical beings who enjoy making love. Our sexual needs are sometimes inexhaustible."

Donnay felt a frantic tug between her thighs. "Thanks for the warning."

"It's the decent thing to do since I plan to keep you in bed with me quite a lot after we get married."

She wondered if he was joking, although the look in his eyes said otherwise. "Do I have a choice in the matter?"

His smile was amusing. "I guess you could always claim a headache, but I doubt that you would want to."

For some reason she doubted it as well, although she would never admit it to him. He was too sure of himself already.

"You know what?" he asked, breaking into her thoughts.

She heard the serious tone in his voice. "What?"

"I'm tired of talking."

A lump formed in Donnay's throat. She'd figured that sooner or later he would be.

"And if you plan on leaving, now is the time to do so because I told you what happens if you stay," he added.

She didn't move. She didn't say anything. She just stood there and stared at him. The more she stared, the more his gaze was touching her all over, making her feel hot and bothered, pushing her over the edge of her control.

And then he tipped the scales when he said in a voice too sexy for words, "Chardonnay Russell, soon to become Chardonnay Westmoreland, welcome to my world of forbidden passion."

He extended his hand out to her while locking his gaze on hers. She thought of everything he said he would do to her if she stayed and knew once she gave her hand to him, she would become his. For some reason that thought didn't bother her as it once had.

Inhaling deeply she placed her hand in his and watched his eyes darken even more before taking her hand and lifting it to his lips to kiss her fingers. And then he was slowly pulling her into his arms and taking her mouth with an intensity that would have brought her to her knees had his hands not wrapped around her waist.

His strength became the overt force that sustained her, the given power that was unconcealed and unrestrained. A shiver raced through her entire being when his tongue mated with hers in a way different from before. This was one of care, custody and control. He was placing ownership all over her mouth, claiming every breath she took and making the moans erupting forth from her throat totally his. The effect was enthralling, sensuously spellbinding and shockingly blazing.

Then she felt his hand working at the zipper at her waist, and moments later when he stepped back slightly without breaking the kiss, she felt her skirt slide down her hips to pool at her ankles. She was left in her blouse, a half-slip and a thong. And as she very well knew, this man had amazing fingers and definitely knew how to use them. He could strip a woman naked before she realized he was doing so. She then felt him slide his hand beneath the waistband of her slip to palm her almost bare bottom.

The moment he touched her, she moaned into his mouth and instinctively her body melded to his, felt his hardness, his erection, and the center of his arousal. He was taking more than she had been prepared to give, was priming her for what was yet to come and fanning a need within her to flashpoint. So she did the only thing she could. She let go.

Then suddenly he pulled back and swept her into his arms. Taking the stairs two at a time he entered the bedroom and placed her on the king-size bed. Her heart began beating faster, almost out of control, when he quickly worked at the buttons of his shirt.

Watching him, studying his eyes, she detected a hunger he was holding in check for now. Her mind began twirling with questions as to what could or would happen if he were to ever let go. She didn't want to think how he would overwhelm her if that were to happen.

He removed his shirt and tossed it on the other side of the room and her breath caught. His chest was so beautifully carved that she felt a moment of intense pride. This was the naked chest that would touch her own each time they made love, skin to skin; the chest she would rub her face in whenever she wanted to inhale the essence of his scent. And his shoulders, broad and firm, were the ones she would cling to when that explosion happened. And for a reason she didn't understand, she had believed him when he'd said it would.

A shiver racked Donnay's body when Spencer's hand went to the zipper of his pants. She held her breath as he eased it down, felt a lump form in her throat when he lowered his pants down his legs and stepped out of them. She finally released her breath and stared at him, her gaze more concentrated than before. It swept past his shoulders and chest to the area hidden by the black silk boxer shorts. The impression showed a very well-endowed man, a man who had everything to back up all the talk, and she believed he knew how to use everything he was packing.

She focused on that part of him that would soon connect their bodies, their minds, their entire beings. In the short time she knew him, she had come to realize that he didn't take too many things lightly. He was intense, demanding, a highly unmanageable person. But on the other hand, she believed he was fiercely dedicated. He would not deceive her like Robert had done.

"What are you thinking?"

His words broke the silence and she looked up to his face. She decided to be only half truthful. "I was wondering how I would handle you. Handle *it*."

He smiled at that. "You see both as a challenge?"

She blew out a breath. If only he knew. "Yes."

"Don't."

Evidently changing his mind about removing his briefs just yet, he moved back to the bed and pulled her up on her knees toward him and then bent down and captured her mouth in one smooth sweep. Something stirred the air surrounding them. She felt it as his tongue began mating with hers again. She felt it when his hands went to her blouse, when he broke the kiss just long enough to pull it over her head. And then he was easing her back into the bed, into the soft, thick cushions of the bedcovers, and straddling her body.

He pulled back and with a quick flick of his wrist and ready fingers, he removed her slip, thong and bra. Before she could inhale a deep breath, his lips were trailing a path down her body, continuing without pause until he reached the twin globes of her breasts. He began kissing them, devouring them, taunting them with his tongue, lips and teeth until she was moaning from deep within her throat. Desire set her ablaze when moments later his mouth began moving again, downward past her ribs and toward her navel. There he discovered her one moment of liberation during her first year in college. A belly ring.

He lifted his head, met her gaze and a broad smile touched his lips. She couldn't help but return his smile and at that moment something significant had passed between them. Acceptance of each other's likes, dislikes and values.

He lowered his head and her stomach tensed when he formed a ring on her belly with his tongue, a hot, wet one that seemed to brand her skin. And then he angled his head as his mouth began moving lower. She stiffened when he kissed the undersides of both her thighs while he reached down to let his fingertips trace a path along her calf.

She heard him murmur words that sounded foreign to her befuddled mind just seconds before he placed the other hand between her thighs to open her legs to him. And then she felt him there, his tongue touching her intimately in a way that lifted her hips off the bed. Her action only seemed to serve his purpose when he took the liberty to lift those same hips closer to his mouth and plunge his tongue inside her, even going so far to raise her legs over his shoulders for deeper penetration.

What he was doing was shooting sensation through her so intensely she felt every part of her shattering. With every flick of his tongue she felt a tug at her insides, as he deliberately pulled everything out of her, every single resistance, every rebellious thought. The feeling was excruciating, intense, unbelievably erotic. She reached out and gripped his shoulders, powerful and strong, and held on for dear life when he demanded anything and everything she was holding back from him.

And then she felt it. A wild, uninhibited dive into waters she had never been in before. But instead of drowning she was caught up on a wave so electrifying, she groaned deep within her throat before screaming out his name.

"Spencer!"

He refused to let up. His tongue went on in a frenzy,

as out of control as she was, and she arched her back as an explosion ripped through her. She felt every muscle in her body take a hit as she moved relentlessly against his mouth, unable to remain still.

She experienced a sense of loss when he pulled back and watched through glazed eyes when he shifted to pull off his boxers. And then he was there, straddling her, and in one swift, smooth move he entered her. Her body's reaction to his invasion was spontaneous. Flesh against flesh, he moved and she moved with him, every thrust as potent, deep and overpowering as the one before. Skin against skin, he slid against her, interlocking their limbs in a hold that was meant to go unbroken, uninterrupted, and unremitting. Any boundaries she'd established were shattered, totally demolished under the powers of his torrid lovemaking.

And then it happened again, another explosion tearing through her. She called out his name a second time, at the same moment he called out hers. And again she felt her body explode, shoot to the stars and beyond. Before she could gather her wits, Spencer's mouth covered hers in a long, slow and drugging kiss that erased all logical thought from her mind.

And she became caught up in Spencer's forbidden passion once again.

What woke Donnay was the feel of a masculine hand running along the side of her thigh, a slow and gentle caress. She slowly opened her eyes. And if she had any doubt just where she was, the hardness of the naked body pressed up against her own was a stark reminder.

She lay there knowing Spencer's hand was intent on

serving a very sensuous purpose; one she had come to expect since last night. He had warned her that when it came to making love he had inexhaustible energy, and over the past three hours he had proven that to be true. The man was so disturbingly virile she hadn't been sure she would be able to keep up. Surprisingly she had. There hadn't been a time when he had reached out for her that she hadn't willingly gone into his arms, knowing the pleasures that awaited her there. And at no time had she been disappointed. Each and every love-making session with him had left her totally and completely satisfied.

When she felt his hand ease between her legs and his efficient fingers went to work, she softly moaned his name.

"I see you're awake," he whispered, rising up on an elbow to gaze down at her.

She looked up at his naked chest, broad and muscular with a spray of dark hair. She remembered burying her face in that chest, taking her tongue and tracing a trail over it when he had been making love to her in one hell of a unique position. The man not only had an infinite amount of energy, he was also very creative. "Did you really expect me to sleep?" she asked, switching her gaze to his face and almost drowning in the depths of his dark eyes.

He smiled and that single smile, sexy to the bone, sent tingles through her body. "I didn't want you to get into any trouble."

She raised a brow. "Trouble?"

"Yes, it's rather late. And as much as I would love for you to stay here with me all night, I don't want to get on your grandmother's and mother's bad side by not returning you home at a decent hour."

She glanced over at the clock on the nightstand. It was already close to two in the morning. She couldn't help but chuckle. "Just what do you consider decent?"

His own voice was slightly amused when he said, "Anytime before daybreak."

Donnay inwardly shivered when his fingers began caressing her womanly core, making her hot and wet again. "Um, you don't have anything to worry about. Grammy is spending the night at the hospital and Mom is meeting a girlfriend in San Francisco and staying overnight. So I would have been home alone anyway."

His fingers went still, and he leaned in closer to her. "Are you saying that you can stay all night?"

She met his gaze and saw the intensity in it as well as the deep rooted desire. It did something to her to know that even after making love several times tonight he still hadn't gotten enough of her. Robert was always eager to send her away from his apartment afterward. Of course she later found out why. She nodded. "Yes, that's exactly what I'm saying."

His expression indicated her words had pleased him and he had no intention of letting her leave his bed now…which was fine with her.

When he lowered his head she was ready and parted her lips the moment he touched them, immediately becoming caught up in the throes of the passion he could generate so effortlessly.

From somewhere deep inside, she was suddenly struck with a terrifying realization. If she wasn't careful and protective of her heart, she could very easily fall in love with Spencer Westmoreland.

Nine

The following morning, Donnay awakened to the loud sound of some sort of heavy machinery. She got out of bed, grabbed Spencer's shirt and slipped it on while quickly walking over to the window to peek out. The sun was just coming up over the horizon, and from a distance across the wide expanse of the vineyard she could see huge construction trucks making their way down the road toward the winery.

"I see Steve's men are on time as usual."

She swung around to see Spencer coming out of the bathroom. It was obvious that he had taken a shower. A towel was tied at his waist, and there were beads of water on his shoulders and chest. She narrowed her eyes and tried not to recall the role his shoulders and chest had played in their lovemaking during the night. There were more important matters to be concerned with right now. "What are those trucks doing here, Spencer?"

He walked over to the dresser, pulled a few items of clothing out of the drawer before dropping the towel. "I think it's obvious what they're doing here, Chardonnay."

She inhaled sharply the moment the towel hit the floor. He was standing before her stark naked and she was trying hard not to stare as he casually slipped into a pair of briefs. She had seen his nude body all last night and during the predawn hours, but seeing it in the bright sunlight was another thing altogether. The memory of all the things that body had done to her, shared with her, made sensations flood her insides. She shook her head and tried to clear her mind of such wanton thoughts and shift it back to what he'd said. "Well, it's not obvious, so tell me," she said.

He glanced over at her. "Those trucks belong to the company I hired to do the expansion to the vineyard."

She became livid. "How dare you!"

He raised a dark brow questioningly and leaned back against the dresser. "How dare I what?"

"How dare you take over. What gives you the right to make such a move without discussing it with any member of my family? We aren't married yet and already you're—"

"I discussed it with your grandfather."

Donnay locked her mouth shut but only for a second. "My grandfather?" she asked in a voice that had suddenly gone soft.

"Yes."

"Are you telling me that you told my grandfather everything about our arrangement?"

"Of course not. During our visits, he talked and I listened, which is a good thing because he shared his dreams with me for the winery. I took in all that he said. He was giving me the big picture—his hopes and dreams. I took it and consulted the best architect I know, and decided to try to make your grandfather's wants viable. Tonight, after telling him we would be getting married, I told him I would make his dream come true."

Donnay stared and then frowned. She didn't recall him saying anything like that to her grandfather. "When did you tell him this?"

"After you left the room to get him a blanket from the nurses' station."

She paused, tilted her head to one side as she considered his words and then asked softly. "And what did he say?"

"Thank you."

Every fiber in Donnay's body wanted to cry. She of all people knew just how long her grandfather had dreamed of expanding the winery, and how depressed he'd been the first time he had become ill and had seen those dreams slip through his fingers when the money for them was needed elsewhere. No one had to tell her that Spencer was giving her grandfather his life back, a reason to get better, a reason to want the surgery he'd been hesitant about having.

She met Spencer's gaze. "It seems I owe you an apology."

"Another one?"

He was standing in nothing but a pair of black briefs, in a sexy stance with his legs braced apart and his arms folded across his chest. From his expression it was obvious he was pretty annoyed with her for jumping to conclusions again. "Well, what was I supposed to think?" she asked in her own defense.

"I can tell you what you weren't supposed to think. The worst about me."

Okay, maybe she shouldn't have, but she had. What did he expect considering the reason he was in their lives? Their marriage would be nothing but a business deal.

As if reading her mind, he said, "I'm a man of my word, Chardonnay."

She slowly crossed the room to him. "And I'm a woman who doesn't have a problem admitting when she's wrong."

"And you're admitting it?" he asked when she came to a stop in front of him.

"Yes, on some things about you," she said, steadily holding his gaze.

He lifted a dark brow. "And the others?"

She shrugged her shoulders. "The jury's still out. But from now on you're innocent until proven guilty."

He caught her wrist and brought it to his lips and kissed it. "It's a good thing for you that I'm a very forgiving man."

"Are you?" she asked in a low tone, feeling heat travel all over her the moment his lips touched her flesh.

"Yes, on some things."

"And the others?"

"The jury is still out. But I don't have a problem with tampering with the jury if it will serve my purpose," he said, reaching out and slipping his shirt off her shoulders to fall in a heap at her feet. She stood before him naked but she had no intention of covering herself. From the look in his eyes, he evidently liked what he saw.

And he wanted what he saw. Again.

"You're very smooth," she said silkily, taking a step closer to wrap her arms around his neck and to bring her body close to his. "And you have one hell of an appetite."

"Don't say I didn't warn you," he said, sweeping her off her feet and into his arms to carry her over to the bed.

"I won't," she murmured into his strong, masculine chest.

Hours later after a long and lazy morning of love-making, Donnay and Spencer got dressed and he walked her home. Both her mother and grandmother were there but neither seemed inclined to ask where she had been.

Spencer then went to talk to Ray Stokes, the foreman for Carr Construction Company. Fred Akron, the architect he had paid, would be presenting his plans for the expansion of the winery by the end of the week. In the meantime, Ray and his crew's job was to clear land to extend the boundaries of the vineyard. Come spring they would be planting more grapevines for more wines to market.

It was way past noon when Spencer returned to the villa, and the moment he opened the door, memories of the night before assailed his mind when he picked up Chardonnay's lingering scent. It seemed to be all over the place. And he liked it. He had drunk chardonnay numerous times but never had he got the taste like he had last night. Good wine was supposed to have a lingering effect, get absorbed into your tongue, your mouth, your flavor palates. He licked his lips, still able to savor her taste on his tongue. Delicious.

He heard his cell phone ring and immediately pulled it out of his pocket. He glanced at the number. It was his brother Ian. Ian was the fraternal twin to his brother Quade and had gotten married that past June. Spencer fondly referred to his brother, who was six years his junior, as the gambler, since he had this unique ability to beat the odds, whether it was poker, a slot machine or blackjack. No one liked playing against Ian since he was known to walk away with everybody's money. He owned a casino and resort in Lake Tahoe, but if you were to ask Ian, his most prized possession was his wife, Brooke.

"And to what do I owe this honor?" Spencer asked teasingly. Since getting married Ian seldom called, saying his time was spent doing more important things. Spencer could just imagine what those other things were.

"Just checking to see if you're still living. Stuart was here at the resort last week and said something about how bad he felt about sending you to face a scorpion."

Spencer chuckled, wondered how Stuart would handle it when he found out that he would be marrying Chardonnay. "It's not that bad," he said and decided Ian would be the first family member he broke his news to. "In fact, it's pretty good. Her name is Char-donnay and I'm marrying her."

There was a pause and then, "You're joking, right?"

"No."

"You're marrying a woman name Chardonnay? Who would name their child after a wine?"

Spencer smiled. "Someone who owns a winery I would imagine."

"You're serious about getting married?"

"Yes. I'm giving the family a call later today. Your call was perfect timing and as a result, you're the first to know."

"When did you meet her?"

"A few weeks ago."

"Um, love at first sight?"

"No." The answer was simple, straightforward and true. "You know me better than that."

"Well, I'm one who knows that love can make you do foolish things."

"Possibly. But I'm not in love," Spencer said, being completely honest with his brother.

"Then why are you getting married? She can't be pregnant already."

Ian's words reminded Spencer that they hadn't used protection any of the times he and Chardonnay had made love last night. That thought didn't bother him since he wanted babies, plenty of them. "I'm getting married because I want to be married. Why let you, Jared and Durango have all the fun? Besides, Mom gets to put another smile on her face."

"But that won't stop her from going after Reggie and Quade," Ian advised.

"No," Spencer agreed. "But they're big boys. They'll have to handle Sarah Westmoreland as they see fit."

He glanced at his watch and saw it was almost two in the afternoon. He wanted to visit Chardonnay's grandfather and give him a report on today's activities. "Look, Ian, there's somewhere I need to be in about an hour. Keep your lips sealed about my upcoming marriage. I want to be the one to tell everyone."

"Okay, my lips are sealed…until such time as I use them to kiss my beautiful wife."

Spencer rolled his eyes heavenward. "Whatever." He then clicked off the phone.

* * *

"The two of you are marrying within two weeks? Why the rush?"

Donnay's looked at Spencer sitting beside her at the dinner table, wondering how he would respond to her mother's question. Not surprisingly, he met her mother's eyes and in a clear voice he said, "Because I don't want to wait."

She expected her grandmother or mother to ask, "Wait for what?" Instead both nodded their heads as if they understood his meaning.

She rolled her eyes. If they did she certainly didn't. It couldn't be that he couldn't wait for them to sleep together since they'd already done that. So the only thing she could figure was that he was anxious to get her pregnant since he was so gung-ho on starting a family.

"I think it's romantic."

Donnay's lips pressed together as she ignored her grandmother's words. Did she really think that or was she just in an extremely good mood because Donnay's grandfather would be coming home from the hospital at the end of the week? She felt Spencer's eyes on her and turned her head to meet his gaze. Fire immediately shot through her veins at the look he was giving her. She figured he was wondering why she had deliberately made herself scarce over the past couple of days. She'd had no choice because otherwise, she would fall deeper and deeper under his spell. And what was more pathetic than for a woman to fall for man who had no intention of ever falling for her?

"Daniel is going to be very pleased with all the work those men are doing on the vineyard," Donnay heard her grandmother say.

Spencer dropped his gaze from hers to look across the table at Catherine Russell. "I hope that he will be. I tried to follow his exact specifications."

Donnay would be the first to admit that he had. She knew that Spencer visited her grandfather daily and always kept him abreast of what was going on with the vineyard. One day she had walked into the hospital room to find her grandfather sitting up in bed with a bunch of architectural plans across his lap while he and Spencer had their heads together, making additional plans.

They'd been so absorbed in their discussion that they hadn't noticed her presence. For a moment she had felt the closeness of the two men and suddenly knew how her mother had felt all those years ago. It was as if Spencer had become the grandson Daniel never had. Not knowing how she felt about that, as well as the other emotions she'd begun feeling around Spencer, she'd decided the best thing to do was to stay clear of him while she screwed her head back on right.

After dinner while clearing the table, Spencer approached her when her mother and grandmother had left to take an evening walk. She'd been hoping that he'd accompanied them and soon discovered he hadn't.

"Okay, what's wrong, Chardonnay?" he asked, his voice low, strained and concerned.

For a moment she couldn't reply. What could she say? I'm falling in love with you and I refuse to do so and will do whatever it takes to make sure it doesn't happen? Instead she shrugged. "What makes you think something is wrong?"

"You've been avoiding me."

She decided to pretend she didn't know what he was talking about. "Avoiding you in what way?"

"You haven't been back to the villa."

Did the man expect her to seek him out and tumble in his bed every chance she got? Her stomach knotted upon remembering his ferocious sexual appetite and concluded that yes, he probably did.

"I've been busy," she responded, both angry and frustrated. They hadn't been alone but a few minutes and already she could feel heated tension sizzle in the very air they were breathing.

"Come to me at midnight," he whispered in a voice tinged with throaty sexuality. He moved closer and drew her to him.

She didn't think of pulling back and although she was trembling inside, she did manage to say, "No."

"Yes," he countered hotly. And then his mouth swooped down on hers before any further protest could come from her lips. The moment his tongue entered her mouth, she remembered, she relented and she surrendered. Every nerve in her body began quivering under Spencer's skillful tongue. The hand he had placed at her waist wasn't helping matters. It only pulled her closer, making her more aware of his powerful heat.

When he finally lifted his head, he had to tighten his hold to keep her from falling. "I won't go to sleep until you get there," he whispered hotly against her lips.

She gazed at him thinking that he wouldn't be going to sleep after she got there, either. There was no doubt in her mind that he intended to keep her awake and busy.

He leaned down and took her lips in his again and then she wasn't thinking at all.

* * *

Donnay couldn't sleep.

She had tossed and turned most of the night. Her body felt hot. It was sensitive. It was experiencing a need to get physical. She kicked back the bedcovers, got out of bed and began pacing the floor. Spencer Westmoreland had gotten under her skin and as much as she tried she couldn't get him out. As a result, she was torn between what she wanted to do and what she knew she should. She had underestimated Spencer.

The man was turning out to be the exact opposite of what she'd assumed he would be. Of course there was a brashness about him she wouldn't even try to discount. But there was also a sense of caring. Her grandfather was proof of that. It wasn't just the time he'd spent with him, but also the fact that he had shared plans of the expansion with her grandfather when he really didn't have to. And then he'd gone further by giving him peace of mind that the vineyard would remain in the Russell family. She had begun seeing another side of Spencer, and with it she felt a grudging respect for him and everything he was doing to be fair to her family.

And she felt something else, something she could no longer deny. Love. She loved him. She sighed. She would marry him, bear his children and make him a good wife. And she hoped and prayed that one day he would grow to reciprocate her love.

A glance at the clock on the nightstand told her that midnight was approaching. She wondered what Spencer was doing. Was he in his bed thinking about her? Waiting on her? Wanting her?

That thought triggered chills that traveled down her

spine. She took a few steps over to her closet and moments later she was slipping out of her nightgown and pulling a skirt and blouse over her head, not bothering with a bra and panties. The outfit was simple, easy to get out of and even a bit sexy. A few moments later after easing her feet into a pair of sandals, she opened her bedroom door and quietly slipped out.

Spencer refused to sleep.

He was feeling restless and positively filled with a need that only Chardonnay could quench. He glanced over at the clock on the wall. It was getting close to midnight. What if he'd pushed too hard and she didn't come? He breathed in deeply, refusing to consider that possibility.

He had spoken to his mother earlier and had given her his news. As expected, she had asked questions, but nothing had stopped her from being elated. Another one of her sons was getting married and she was tickled pink. He knew by tomorrow morning the entire Westmoreland clan would hear about it. He would get calls, probably more questions—especially from his brothers and cousins who knew how his mind operated—but that thought didn't bother him. Like he'd told his mother, Chardonnay was the woman he wanted and the woman he intended to marry here in the vineyard in two weeks.

A sense of accomplishment rolled over him as he thought of having the things that were most important to him. The most significant one at the moment was Chardonnay. He thought of her often, even times when he didn't want to. What he'd told her mother at dinner was the truth. The reason he wanted to rush into marriage was that he didn't want to wait … mainly to make her his.

Deciding if she were to come to him he preferred her not making the trip from the main house through the vineyard alone, he slid out of bed and slipped into the jeans and shirt he had on earlier. His skin felt hot to the touch and he wondered if the same heat consuming his body was consuming hers. When he'd kissed her earlier that night, he had felt her response, had tasted her desire, inhaled her heat.

He wanted it.

He needed it.

His mind was becoming mentally shaken, his body physically addicted. They had made love one night, numerous times over, and that was all it had taken to reduce him to a man who stayed royally aroused around her. A man who spent most of his day dealing with frustrated lust. As he left the bedroom and began walking down the stairs his mind was filled with one thing and one thing only. Making love to Chardonnay.

Moments later he was closing the front door behind him as he made his way down the path. It was dark and the only light was from the moon overhead. The night air was cool and he wished he had thought to grab a jacket. It had rained earlier, right after he had returned home. It hadn't rained a lot, but enough to dampen the earth, supplying a distinctive aroma of wet grass, blooming plants, thickening vines and the earthy fragrance of freshly turned soil.

Feeling his fingers go cold, he hooked them in the pockets of his jeans. He suddenly sharpened his gaze when he heard a rustling sound. Thinking it was Chardonnay, he was about to call out to her then stopped after seeing it was her mother instead. Then before he could blink, another figure—that of a tall, muscular man— stepped out of the shadows and into the moonlight in front of her.

Spencer's protective instincts kicked in and his senses immediately went on full alert. Then he watched as the man pulled Ruth Russell into his arms and kissed her, and it was quite obvious she was kissing him back.

Spencer lowered his head, not wanting to intrude on such a passionate moment between the couple who, like him, were meeting for a midnight rendezvous. Moments later he glanced up in time to see them disappear into the shadows heading in the direction of the empty gardener's cottage.

Not that it was any of his business, but he wondered if Chardonnay knew that her mother was involved in an affair. If she didn't, she definitely wouldn't hear about it from him. When it came to secrets, he was the king of discreet. Still he couldn't help but wonder about the man's identity. Was he one of the workers at the winery?

Fairly certain the couple was halfway to their chosen destination by now, he began walking again. The night was quiet so he easily picked up the sound of footsteps coming his way. He stopped and focused his gaze. And then he saw her.

She hadn't seen him yet so he leaned back against an oak tree to study her features in the moonlight. Beautiful. And then his body began thrumming at the realization that although he was fairly certain she hadn't wanted to come, desire had driven her to seek him out.

Something gave him away. Possibly the sudden intake of his breath when he saw her outfit. It was one of those fit-and-flare skirts and a jersey-knit top with billowy sleeves. The way they clung to her body sent a surge of adrenaline pumping through his veins. She stopped walking and stared at him and he pushed away from the tree and strolled toward her.

He had spent the last three hours wondering if she would show up, and now that she was here, his already hot blood was boiling even more at the thought of how they would spend the rest of their time together. He wasn't used to a woman taking control of his thoughts like she was doing.

"You came," were the only words he could fix his mouth to say at that moment, he was so filled with un-leashed passion.

"Yes, I came," she whispered, and the sound sent his insides to quivering. He battled the urge to take her then and there, to let their naked bodies roll in the damp earth, get tangled in the vines and—"

"It's cool out."

He saw her rubbing her arms and quickly realized that like him she hadn't worn a jacket. He smiled a tight, restrained smile. Anything else would cause the erection to burst in his crotch. "Then let's go to my place where I can warm you. But that's not all I plan to do to you tonight, Chardonnay."

Her incredible gray eyes gazed deeply at him when she asked in a soft, sexy voice, "What else do you plan to do to me?"

She had a right to ask. She had a right to know. "Taste every single inch of you. Let my fingers stroke you. Let my body make love to you in all kinds of ways and various positions."

He took a step closer to her. "Will you let me do all those things to you again?"

"Yes."

Pleased she hadn't hesitated with her answer, he dipped his head and tasted her lips, savoring his own special brand of Chardonnay. He lifted his mouth, deciding he needed to take her to a place more private before he lost control. The last thing he wanted was for her mother to come upon them like he had on her earlier.

"When you leave my bed tonight I want you to be totally and thoroughly convinced that I am the only man you'll ever want and need." And then he swung her up into his arms and began walking back toward his villa.

He had gotten halfway there and couldn't go anymore. The feel of her in his arms, the way her breasts were pressed against chest, the scent of her in his nostrils, the way she had tucked her hands beneath his shirt to keep them warm, all of them increased his sexual craze. He couldn't move another inch without the threat of his aroused body exploding then and there.

Inhaling deeply, he placed her on her feet. She gazed at him for a moment and then as if understanding what he couldn't put into words, she took his hand and said, "Come with me. I want to show you something."

She led him through a thicket of low-hanging branches, parting several grapevines that blocked their way, to guide him to a grassy path. There at the end of it was a glass enclosed summerhouse, sitting amidst vines, ferns, a cluster of oak trees and palms. She glanced at his expression. He didn't even try to hide his smile.

"Gramps had it built years ago for my grandmother, a place where she could get away, sew, read and rest. She hasn't used it much over the years. It's climate controlled and should be nice and warm inside," she said, opening the door. He followed her inside and then she locked it behind them. It was nice and warm on the inside and the window blinds assured complete privacy.

After she turned on a lamp, he glanced around but only for a second. His gaze immediately returned to her when he saw the frown bunching her brow. "What is it?" he asked.

"Um, nothing, I guess. It's just that no one ever comes out here but me to read and take a nap on occasion. However, it seems the bedcovers have been changed since the last time I was here."

Spencer had an idea who had changed the bedcovers but kept his thoughts to himself. "Does it matter?"

She met his gaze and shook her head. "No. Nothing matters but this moment. With you."

Something tugged deep inside of him. He could not deny the sensation even if he wanted to. Even if he didn't fully understand it. He opened his arms to her and she took the few steps to walk into them. Instinctively she lifted her head and at the same time he lowered his, covering her lips.

A ferocious ache overtook him and he whispered words against her lips, not sure what he was saying and at the moment not caring. The only thing that mattered to him was the ravenous desire running rampant through his entire body. She arched against him and his senses went into overdrive.

Like a man with no control, he stepped back and

tugged her blouse over her head. The moment he saw her braless, he closed his hand over her breasts, reveling in their shape, their firmness and how right they felt in his hands. He then leaned down and kissed them, satisfying his hungry need to taste her.

But he soon discovered it wasn't enough for him.

He dropped to his knees in front of her and tugged her skirt down her thighs and almost swallowed his tongue when he stared her feminine mound smack in the face. She hadn't worn panties.

He leaned forward to do his own taste test as his nose nuzzled the curls at the apex of her thighs, taking in her scent, letting his nostrils absorb her aroma just seconds before his tongue thrust deep inside her while grabbing hold of her bottom, pulling her closer to the fit of his mouth. He became lost in heavenly bliss while his tongue stroked, caressed and probed, refusing to let up or let go. He heard her moans, felt the torture on his shoulders when her fingernails dug into them, but he refused to release her from his grip.

This was his Chardonnay and he intended to enjoy it to the fullest. Even when he felt her body explode beneath his mouth he held tight, needing to fully taste the very essence of her.

It was only after the last tremor had left her body that he drew back from the intimate kiss. He glanced up at her, met the dazed gray of her eyes and a smile curved his mouth as he licked his lips. "Best Chardonnay I've ever had the pleasure of tasting," he whispered before standing and sweeping her naked body off her feet and into his arms.

He carried her over to the daybed and placed her on

it and then quickly began removing his clothes. It had started raining again, a downpour that beat against the rooftop and glass walls. The air seemed to thicken with the fragrance of flowers, grapes and sex. He inhaled it. He licked his lips and could still taste it. He was suddenly filled with a sexual rush, a need to mate to an extreme he never thought possible. He wanted her. Damn, how he wanted her.

He moved back toward the bed. Instead of wrapping her arms around his neck like he assumed she would do, she grabbed hold of his shaft and stroked the head of his erection with soft fingers. In his already sexually glazed mind that was the last thing he needed but exactly what he wanted. Her touch was eliciting sounds from his throat, and he felt himself weaken, giving in to the demands of his body. The demands of her hands.

He felt her touch all the way to his bones, felt himself harden even more beneath her fingertips. She mentally fractured any thoughts he had, igniting a fuse within him that could explode any minute. And when she pushed him back on the bed and took him into her mouth, he clenched his jaw to keep from hollering. He gripped the bedcovers as her mouth began ravaging him, sapping him of any strength while at the same time seizing the air in his lungs. Sensations swamped him and he gave himself up to them, and to her.

Good God! What was she doing to him? He had to stop her before he was stripped of everything within him. A deep moan escaped his lips when he shifted and pushed her on her back, locking his thighs over hers, trapping her beneath him. Before she could mutter a single word of protest, he entered her and they both released moans of pleasure at the same time, just seconds before they began spiraling out of control.

He reached under her and lifted her hips as he thrust in and out of her, and with each stroke she arched her body to meet him, creating a sensuous blend of perfect harmony.

"Incredible," he murmured, just seconds before dipping his head to her mouth, laving her lips with his tongue from corner to corner before inserting his tongue into her mouth. Below he felt her inner muscles clench him, milk him, attempt to pull everything out him, and she succeeded.

"Chardonnay!"

His body seemed to explode in tiny pieces as his seed spilled deep inside her, overflowing within her and over-whelming him. Never before had he given so much to any woman and with no regrets and no restraints. That thought became logged in his brain but he refused to dwell on it now. The only thing he wanted to think about was how he felt inside her and how his body was still throbbing from the effects of the most intense orgasm he'd ever experienced.

Their gazes connected and he felt like he was sinking in quicksand. He clung to her, afraid if he let go that would be the end of it…of them.

As he pulled her shaking body closer to him, more sensations shot through him and at that moment, he couldn't fathom a life without the woman in his arms.

Donnay came awake to discover Spencer gazing down at her. She blinked, wondering how long she'd slept. The last thing she remembered was coming apart in his arms while he was buried deep inside of her, feeling the heated essence of him shooting to all parts of her.

"I have something for you," he whispered huskily.

His words made her study his features. "What?"

"This."

And then she felt him slip something onto her finger, and she knew what it was. Her engagement ring. The huge diamond shone brightly in the moonlight and Donnay's breath caught. It was exquisite, the most beautiful ring she'd ever seen.

Not knowing what to say, she sank against him instead and he pulled her into his arms and held her. She knew that loving Spencer when he didn't love her back wouldn't always be easy. He was a hard man, a man who'd been hurt by love. It would be up to her to go about repairing his heart mainly because she believed in the very essence of her soul that it was a heart worthy of fixing.

"It's beautiful, Spencer," she finally said. "Simply beautiful. Thank you."

"You're welcome." Then he said, "The rain has stopped. Are you ready to get dressed and go to my place?"

She looked at him. Her heart was assured that although he didn't love her, he definitely wanted her. "Yes," she said, wrapping her arms around his neck. "I'm ready."

Ten

Spencer stood at the window in his bedroom and glanced out. It had been four days since he'd told his mother about his wedding plans and his phone was still ringing. His cousin Delaney had even called him all the way from her home in the Middle East to congratulate him.

He leaned against the windowsill, thinking the last few days had been sheer bliss. Chardonnay seemed to have accepted the way things would be between them and no longer fought the idea that in less than two weeks they would be getting married.

And their relationship had definitely improved. They were now an engaged couple and instinctively acted the part. They had begun sharing breakfast and dinner each day, would take walks together in the afternoon while he brought her up-to-date on that day's work activities, and at night they shared a bed. He no longer had to seduce her to do so. Each night she would come to him automatically, as though she knew her place was beside him in bed, and a part of him felt that it was.

Last night they had attended a wine-tasting gala in downtown Napa, Taste Napa Downtown. The outfit Chardonnay had worn had been both professional and seductive. and he had felt proud to be the man at her side. When they'd entered the ballroom where the event had been held, heads had turned and more than one person had commented that they made a striking couple.

On that thought he lowered his head as a deep sensation settled in his gut, one he'd tried ignoring over the past few days. Whenever he was with Chardonnay, whether in bed or out, he felt like a different person, a man on top of the world. A man who was starting to live for the first time. To appreciate the finer things in life. A man who was looking forward to his future.

A man who was in love.

His breath paused in his throat. Falling in love was something he never intended to happen to him, but it had. He rubbed his hand over his face, accepting what his heart had been trying to tell him lately, but what he had ignored until now.

Months ago, if anyone would have suggested that he'd give his heart to any woman, he would have laughed in their face, knowing such a thing wasn't possible. But he was living proof that it was possible.

He glanced out the window again when he heard the equipment plowing the earth to cultivate additional land for grapes to be planted in the spring. He was anticipating a good harvest in the coming year and was anticipating becoming a father in that time as well. But more than anything he wanted to be a good husband to Chardonnay, and he hoped that in time she would get over the circumstances of their marriage and accept the fact · they were together and build on that.

Her grandfather had got out of the hospital a few days ago and Spencer found he was spending time with the older man as well. Daniel's health was improving and he'd been extremely happy to come home and discover his plans and dreams for the winery were coming true. To avoid tiring the older man out, the architect Spencer had hired was meeting with Daniel a couple of hours a day to make sure the plans being drawn were exactly the way Chardonnay's grandfather had envisioned them.

Spencer turned when he heard his phone ring, interrupting his thoughts. He moved away from the window and walked over to the desk to pick it up. "Yes?"

"Something interesting has developed that I think you should know about."

Spencer arched a brow at the serious sound of his attorney's voice. "And what is that, Stuart?"

"Over a million dollars was deposited into the Russell Vineyards bank account this morning."

Spencer's body stiffened as his mind began whirling with questions. He took a breath. "There has to be a mistake."

"No mistake, Spence."

"Then how did it get there? Who made the deposit?"

"It was a transfer that I was able to trace from a Korean bank. An international account in the name of BOSS."

Spencer lifted a brow. "Boss?"

"Yes."

He stared at the floor as various things ran through

his mind. He didn't want to consider any of them but knew that he had to. "Find out who owns the account and even more importantly, why they would have deposited that money into the Russells' account?"

"All right. You don't think that Chardonnay Russell borrowed the money elsewhere, even though she knew you'd agreed to front the financing for the expansion, do you?"

He inhaled sharply. That was a possibility he didn't want to consider. Over the past weeks he had let his guard down and had done something he swore he wouldn't after what Lynette Marie had done to him, and that was to begin trusting another woman. Not to mention fall in love.

He had to admit that his mind hadn't been on a lot lately, other than making love to her. A dark suspicion leaped to life inside of him. Had she used his moment of weakness to keep him occupied so he wouldn't find out what she was doing behind his back until it was too late?

"Spence?"

His attorney's voice made him aware he hadn't answered his question. "I'm not sure what's going on, Stuart, but I want you to find out."

"I will and in the meantime, be careful how you handle your business."

Spencer knew Stuart's meaning and as he clicked off the phone a part of him thought that his attorney's advice may have come a little too late.

A few hours later, Spencer snapped closed his luggage and moved away from the bed. Stuart hadn't returned his call. That meant the information they wanted was hard to get, which was usually the case involving international accounts. Why would anyone place that much money into the Russells' account unless someone had negotiated a deal elsewhere? And since Chardonnay was the one handling the family's business, he could only assume it had been her.

Doubt and suspicions he didn't want to feel were eating at him, and he couldn't forget the moment he'd received the coroner's report on Lynette Marie. Betrayal of the worst kind had wretched his insides and as much as he was trying not to let it happen, he was beginning to feel the same way now.

He walked over to the window and looked out at the hills and valleys. Disgust and anger ate at him. Although the circumstances were different, the results were the same. He had allowed another woman to betray him. And this time the pain cut deeper because he loved her.

From the beginning she had alluded that in the end, he would regret ever coming up with the idea for the two of them to marry. He had merely brushed her comment aside as insignificant. But Chardonnay Russell had played him for a fool. She had weaved her deceitful web around him, first in the physical sense and then in an emotional sense. Each and every time they'd made love it had weakened him, had turned him into putty in her hands to the extent that all he'd thought about over the past week—besides marrying her—was pleasing her, making her happy, trying to show her that a lifetime with him wouldn't be so damn awful.

And all the time he'd been working hard doing that, she had been undermining him, setting him up for failure and intentionally messing with his heart.

He turned away from the window when he heard the sound of the key turning in the lock downstairs. It would be Chardonnay. Before she'd left his bed early that morning she'd agreed to return a little before noon to give him a tour of the section of the winery he hadn't yet seen, and to introduce him to all the employees.

He turned back to the window when he heard her footsteps coming up the stairs. Anger consumed him to a degree he hadn't thought possible and it would have definitely been to her benefit if he could have left and returned to Sausalito without seeing her. In his present state of mind, he would have preferred it.

He turned when she opened the door and when his gaze touched hers he felt a hardening deep in his chest. At the same time a sensation of pain surrounded his heart.

"I told you I would be back," she said, smiling and stepping into the room, closing the door behind her.

When he didn't say anything but just stared at her, her gaze shifted to the bed where she saw his packed luggage. He watched as her smile faded. "You have to go away on business?"

He inhaled deeply, not in the mood to play her games, although she evidently assumed he was gullible enough to do so. He moved away from the window and went to stand before her. "Yes, I'm leaving but it's not on business. I'm leaving for good and won't be coming back."

She shook her head as if she hadn't heard him correctly. "But what about the wedding?"

His heart hardened even more when he said, "There won't be a wedding. You would be the last woman I'd marry."

If her reaction was anything to go by, it seemed that

his words had immediately knocked the breath out of her body, sent an invisible slap across her face. She placed a hand over her heart and her eyes widened in shocked disbelief. "Why? I don't understand. What happened?"

Her pretense angered him even more. "Let's cut the bull, Chardonnay, shall we? How long did you think it would be before I found out?"

A confused look appeared on her face. "Found out what?"

Spencer shook his head and laughed, not believing she had the nerve to ask him that. Even now she was standing in front of him with a puzzled expression, as if she had no clue what he was talking about, but he knew otherwise.

"I have to hand it to you. You are one hell of an actress. What did you do to get the money, Chardonnay? Are you sleeping with him like you're sleeping with me?" He watched color drain from her face. Guilt, he thought.

"I don't know what you're talking about," she said in a low, strained voice, shaking her head as if to deny his words.

"Don't you?" he said angrily, his tone bitter. "You want me to believe you have no idea who deposited a million dollars into the winery account this morning?"

"What! A million dollars? You're wrong. There must be a mistake."

He chuckled. "Oh, yes, there's a mistake all right, and it was made the day I set eyes on you."

"No, Spencer, listen to me. There has to be a mistake." She reached out as if to make a plea and he grabbed her wrist firmly in his hand and hauled her tightly against his chest.

His stony gaze met hers. "You played me for a fool, Chardonnay. You never intended to marry me and have my children. You had a plan B all along, didn't you?"

"No, that's not true. How could you think I could be so dishonest and calculating? How could—"

"Enough! I don't want to hear anything you have to say." He released her hand and moved around her and grabbed his luggage off the bed. He headed for the door, paused and then swung around to look at her again. "Tell your grandfather that I will continue to pay those men to clear the additional twenty acres like I promised him I would. I will also take care of any and all expenses associated with any surgery he might have, because deep down I don't believe he knew just what kind of games you were playing, just what a deceitful person you are. And," he said, pausing briefly, "if you're already pregnant with my child then rest assured you haven't seen the last of me. And if you aren't, then I hope to God I never see you again."

He turned around and without looking back again, he left.

"Donnay! What's wrong?" Ruth shot to her feet the moment Donnay entered the house.

Donnay had been hoping her mother had left to go to the winery's gift shop that she supervised and wouldn't see her this way. She hurriedly wiped the tears from her eyes as she moved toward the stairs. None of what Spencer had accused her of made sense. How could he have thought she had deceived him? Although she had called the bank and they had confirmed the million-dollar deposit, she had no idea who had done it, or why.

"Donnay?"

She met her mother's worried gaze and said in a low, shaky voice, "I'm fine, Mom."

"Then why are you crying?"

It took Donnay awhile to compose herself before saying, "Spencer has called off the wedding. He thinks I've deceived him."

Ruth looked stunned. "Deceived him? Why would he think that?"

Donnay tried to still her shaking hands as she wiped another tear from her eye. She was angry and upset. "He thinks I never intended to marry him because I was getting the money I needed to save the winery from someone else. He even suggested I was sleeping with someone else to get it."

"How could he suggest something so despicable?"

"Because someone deposited a million dollars into the winery bank account and I—"

Donnay stopped talking upon her mother's sharp intake of breath. She studied her mother's features. Ruth Russell was flushing guiltily. Something wasn't right and Donnay played her hunch by asking, "Mom, do you know where that money came from? I checked with the bank and it's actually there."

Ruth stared back at her daughter and slowly nodded. "Yes, I know where it came from. He said he was going to do it but I asked him not to, because I believed that everything with you and Spence would work out just fine."

Donnay was having a hard time keeping up with what her mother was saying. She placed a hand on her arm. "He? Who is *he*, Mom?"

Ruth drew in a ragged breath and then she said, "Your father."

Stunned, Donnay could only stare at her mother. Her mind tried denying what her ears had just heard. There had to be a mistake. But something pushed her to ask for clarification purposes. "My father?"

"Yes. I told him about the outlandish proposal Spencer had made to you and Chad said that he—"

"Whoa. Back up a minute, Mom. I'm trying to follow you here but I'm having a hard time. Are you saying you've seen my father? Actually talked to him?"

Ruth nodded again. "Yes, he called a few weeks ago and said he was in the area and wanted to see me."

"In the area?"

"Yes. He was in San Francisco on business and decided to rent a car and come to the valley. He wasn't sure if I was still living here, or if over the years I had married and moved away."

Donnay inhaled. "I guess you got around to telling him about me," she said quietly.

Ruth nodded. "Yes. At first he wasn't happy about having a daughter he'd never known about, was cheated out of knowing. But then I explained to him how those letters came back. I'd even kept them and showed them to him so he'd know that I had tried contacting him."

"So," Donnay said slowly, "what has he been doing all these years? Is he married? Does he have any other children?"

Ruth shook her head. "He's a widower. His wife of fifteen years died five years ago and they never had any children. He retired from the army and went into business for himself; some sort of international electronic corporation that has done well over the years. And now that he knows about you, he wants to meet you, Chardonnay."

Ruth smiled slightly. "You should have seen him that first night after I told him about you. He was ready to come here and claim you immediately, but I convinced him to wait until I felt the time was right. Besides, he and I needed to talk, to find out what has been happening in our lives over the years. When I told him about the winery's problems, and how you were willing to sacrifice your happiness to marry a man you didn't love just to save the winery, he offered to pay off the debt. He said he would put the money into our account as soon as it could be transferred. I asked him not to, but like you he's stubborn and has this protective instinct and he did it anyway. I'm sorry if doing so has caused friction between you and Spencer."

Donnay shook her head after hearing her mother's explanation. "It doesn't matter. Our marriage would have been doomed from the start, Mom. This shows just how little he trusted me, and a marriage not based on faith and trust is no marriage at all. I could have survived without love but I have to know that Spencer has faith in me and trusts me. Without it, a relationship couldn't last."

A small smile touched her lips as the picture became clear in her mind. "So, is my father the *old friend* you've been spending a lot of time with lately?"

Ruth actually blushed. "Yes, and he is very anxious to meet you."

"And I'm anxious to meet him as well." Donnay turned to go up the stairs then, but Ruth's voice held her back.

"He loves you, you know."

"Who, Mom?"

"Spencer."

Donnay chuckled to hold back fresh tears. "No, he never loved me, Mom. Our marriage was going to be a business deal. I told you that."

"Yes, but I have my own eyes, Donnay. That might have been his intent but it didn't last. That night he came for dinner, he couldn't keep his eyes off you. You might not have noticed but your grandmother and I certainly did. Spencer Westmoreland loves you."

Donnay glanced down at her left hand. She had removed her engagement ring and she held it, clenched tightly in her fist. She then looked back up at her mother. "No, Mom, he doesn't love me, but you know what's really sad and probably pathetic? I fell in love with him and was actually looking forward to being his wife and the mother of his children."

Knowing she couldn't hold back her tears much longer, she said, "I think I'll go into town. I need to get away for a while." Then without saying anything else, she raced up the stairs.

Spencer tensed visibly when the phone rang. A part of him knew it had to be Stuart. He placed his wineglass on the table and picked up the house phone.

Arriving home to Sausalito had been a welcome relief. He had spent the past couple of hours opening up windows and blinds to enjoy the view of the Bay from his living-room window. To keep busy he had immediately begun work on another business deal, one that would involve his cousins and brothers. His cousin Clint had retired as a Texas Ranger and was using the ranch he had inherited from his uncle to set up a business much like the one Durango and McKinnon had established.

He picked up the phone. "Yes?"

"I got the information you wanted, Spence."

Spencer remained silent for a moment then said. "All right. Who put that money into the Russell's account?"

"A man by the name of Chad Timberlain."

Spencer racked his mind trying to recall where he'd heard that name before. It suddenly hit him at the same time he heard a knock at his door. He felt a hard tug on his insides at the thought that he might have jumped to the wrong conclusions about Chardonnay.

"Look, Stuart, I'll need to get back to you. I think I know what might be going on, but I'll have to verify it and call you back."

He hung up the phone and headed for the door, wondering who would be visiting him since no one knew he had returned to Sausalito. He snatched opened the door to find a tall, muscular, fifty-something-year-old man standing there.

Spencer inhaled slowly. Although the two of them had never met, he recognized the man's profile as the one he'd seen that night on the path, just seconds before he had taken Ruth Russell into his arms.

"Chad Timberlain?" Spencer caught the man by surprise in asking.

The older man frowned coolly. "Yes."

Spencer stepped aside. "Come in. I really wasn't expecting you, since I just figured things out. But I'm sure you're here because you feel that the two of us need to talk."

The older man gave him a look that indicated the two of them needed to do more than merely exchange words and Spencer understood. If he was in Timberlain's place, he'd do the same thing. "And we need to come to an understanding," Spencer decided to add.

The man's features relaxed somewhat as he stepped over the threshold, and Spencer exhaled as he closed the door behind him.

"So, as you can see," Spencer said sometime later to Chad Timberlain, as they sat in his living room finishing off glasses of Russell wine, "I assumed Chardonnay knew about the money that had been placed in the winery's account.

"Even when she told you she didn't know anything about it?" Chad asked, his gaze boring into Spencer. After the two of them began talking, the older man's manner appeared calm and relaxed. But the more Spencer outlined just what his and Chardonnay's relationship was, the more the conversation between them became somewhat strained. Although Timberlain hadn't been involved in his daughter's life before now, he felt that was neither here nor there since he intended to become involved. Starting here.

There was only one answer Spencer could give and it was one he wasn't really proud of. "Yes, even when she denied my allegations."

The man's gaze hardened under Spencer's direct stare. "I felt compelled to place that money into the account because I couldn't stand there and let you railroad my daughter into marrying you."

After hearing his account of his relationship with

Chardonnay—minus, of course the intimate part—he didn't find her father's attitude the least bit unreasonable. "Yes, sir. I understand and I can also appreciate that."

The man nodded. "So what are you going to do to rectify the situation? Ruth feels that you love Chardonnay and what happened was a grave mistake on your part."

Spencer swallowed. Grave was too mild a word. He couldn't see her ever forgiving him. He had asked her to believe in him and trust him, yet he hadn't done the same for her. He met her father's intense gaze. "I do love your daughter and will be the first to admit I was wrong. If she never speaks to me again I will understand."

He then leaned forward. "But because I love her, I'm going to fight for her and hope that she finds it in her heart to give me another chance. It's no longer about what I can do for the winery, it's about us—Chardonnay and me."

A smile touched the corners of Chad Timberlain's lips. "I've yet to officially meet my daughter, in fact I plan to do so tonight. From what Ruth tells me she can be pretty stubborn at times, so you won't have an easy job."

No one had to tell Spencer about Chardonnay's stubbornness. He was very much aware of it. "I know, but I'm going to die trying," he said, and he meant every word.

Donnay glanced at her reflection in the mirror as she tried to ignore the butterflies in her stomach. She would be meeting her father for the first time tonight. Her heart was already filled with love for him. Without having met her, he had come to her aid by putting that money into the winery account and proving that he would be a father who would always be there for his daughter.

She had hoped that getting caught up in meeting her father would eliminate thoughts of Spencer from her mind. Tomorrow was soon enough to be faced with the task of canceling everything. She would have to call the florist, the caterer and the printer. She wondered if he had told his family yet and if he had, what reason he had given them for calling off the wedding. No doubt he had convinced them—like he was convinced—that she was someone who couldn't be trusted.

She glanced at the clock on the wall. It was nearing six o'clock. Tonight her family would be hosting a small dinner party to celebrate her grandfather's homecoming, as well as her father's entrance back into their lives. Her mother had confided in her earlier that she and Chad Timberlain were doing some serious dating. Donnay was happy knowing there was a chance her mother might be able to recapture the love she had lost over twenty-seven years ago.

She heard a knock on her bedroom door. Thinking it was her mother or grandmother, she said, "Come in."

Donnay turned to see the door open and instead of her mother or grandmother, her breath caught when Spencer walked in. Fierce emotions welled up in her throat when she remembered his harsh words, his accusations. He had asked her to believe in him when he had no intention of ever believing in her. "What are you doing here, Spencer? What do you want?" she asked in an angry tone.

He moved into the room so quickly that she hadn't been given time to blink. When she did, he was standing there, right in front of her. His voice was gentle yet husky when he spoke. "I'm here to apologize for all the things

I said. And as far as what I want…what I want Chardonnay, is you."

All it took was one look at Chardonnay's features to know his apology hadn't softened her any. Anger lined her gray eyes and she was standing stiff, with her hands balled into fists. He noticed that she had removed his ring.

"You accused me of those god-awful things. You played judge and jury. You didn't trust me. You—"

He reached out and tried touching her hand, the one that no longer wore his ring, and she angrily snatched it back. "No! You even accused me of betraying you with another man. How could you think so low of me?"

Spencer saw the tears in her eyes and a deep lump formed in his throat. He had hurt her. He had caused her pain and more than anything he wanted to make it right. "I love you, Chardonnay," he said in a low voice, straight from the heart. "I never meant to fall in love with you but I did. I'm the one who got caught up in all my scheming and manipulative tactics. I have been betrayed before. A few years ago, when my fiancée was killed, I discovered she was pregnant by another man. I made a promise to myself then that although I still wanted a wife and children, there would be no love. But you proved me wrong because you demanded my love without even realizing you were doing it. And when I found out about the money in your account, I felt used and betrayed because I realized you no longer had anything to gain from our marriage and that in essence, you no longer needed me…but I had begun needing you."

Donnay inhaled deeply. Spencer's words from earlier that day had been cruel, unjustified and angry. But now she understood why he had been so quick to judge her falsely. His former fiancée had gotten pregnant by someone else? She couldn't imagine a woman wanting to have any man's baby but his. Even now she was hoping that she was already pregnant.

She saw the strain and pain on Spencer's face. He had admitted that he loved her, which definitely came as a surprise. And she believed him because confessing his love to a woman couldn't be easy for him. And she loved him, too. She loved him with all her heart.

"If I accept your apology, and believe what you say about loving me, what do you expect of me?" she asked in a soft voice.

He placed both hands in the pockets of his pants as he stood gazing at her. "I expect—I would hope that you will take me back, give me another chance to prove just how wrong I've been and to make things right. I would want us to go ahead with our wedding and become husband and wife, but I'll let you set the date. If you prefer waiting until after the holidays then that's fine. I will no longer rush you into anything."

He sighed deeply then continued. "And I would want you to give me a chance to love you in such a way that you would want to love me back. " A smile curved his lips when he added honestly. "I will make it almost impossible for you not to do so. And if you're not pregnant already, then I'll let you decide when we'll have children. I won't make it a priority. I want to spend time with you and love you the way you rightly deserve without any limitations or stipulations imposed."

Donnay didn't say anything for a while and then she tilted her head and studied him. She saw the strain lines across his forehead, the tension that had tightened around his lips. But it was his eyes that brought it all home. They were dark, intense and filled with love…for her. "And what if I were to say that I already love you, that I had fallen in love with you weeks ago?" she asked in a tight voice, fighting back a sob that threatened to close her throat. "What if I were to say that, Spencer?"

He took a step closer to her. "Then I would ask you to give me an opportunity to make you never regret loving me, never regret giving me another chance. Never regret becoming my wife and the mother of my children. Will you?"

She slowly nodded. "Yes."

Happiness spread across his features and he removed his hands from his pockets and reached out for her. This time she didn't deny him and willingly went into his open arms. He held her tightly to him, as if he never intended to let her go, and then he tilted up her chin and captured her mouth with his, glorying in the taste of his own personal brand of Chardonnay.

The moment his tongue took hold of hers, sensations rippled through him, pleasure seeped into his bones and desire filled his entire being. If her family didn't have a number of dinner guests downstairs he would be tempted to lock the door and stay in this bedroom with her forever. Besides, her father would not let him do such a thing. The man had given him twenty minutes before he'd threatened to come up and rescue his daughter, if need be. The only need was the one Spencer felt in his crotch.

"I want to make love to you," he whispered against her moist lips.

"And I want you to make love to me."

He smiled. "Later tonight? At the villa?"

She grinned. "Yes, later tonight. At the villa."

Although he wanted to keep her in her bedroom a little longer, moments later Spencer found himself escorting Chardonnay down the stairs. In just the nick of time, he figured, because standing on the bottom step was her father, waiting on them. Spencer held her hand, the one that once again was wearing his ring.

Spencer stopped in the middle of the staircase and turned to Chardonnay. "This first meeting should be your time with him. Go down to your father."

She smiled when Spencer released her hand, and continued walking alone down the stairs. A grin of pure happiness covered Chad Timberlain's face and he opened his arms up to the daughter he only recently discovered he had. Automatically, she returned the affection by walking straight into his waiting arms.

"Dad," she whispered while he held her tight. Chardonnay glanced across the room and saw her mother standing with her grandparents, tears in their eyes. Tonight was very special. The father she'd never met had come to claim his daughter, and the man she had fallen in love with loved her back.

She felt utterly and truly happy.

Later that night, Donnay lay wrapped up in Spencer's arms. After an intense lovemaking session, they had talked. Since he hadn't called his family to cancel the wedding plans, and she hadn't cancelled the florist, caterer or printer, they decided to still get married the week before Christmas. Besides, each and every time they made love they ran the risk of starting a family, which was something the both of them decided they still wanted to do.

Donnay smiled, thinking about what he'd told her earlier. "I can't believe my father actually came to see you."

"Well, he did and he wanted to let me know in no uncertain terms that he would not tolerate me taking advantage of his daughter."

"He's really special. To think he put all that money into my bank account to help out."

Her father had explained after retiring from the military, he and three guys who'd served under him in the army had formed an international electronic company called BOSS and it was doing extremely well. He had assured her that giving her that much money had not affected the company's bottom line.

Chad was semiretired and the first of the year he planned to step down as CEO and turn over the day-to-day operation of the company to the three competent men whom he considered surrogate sons. Donnay would get to meet them at her wedding.

"So when do you think your mom and Chad will marry?" Spencer asked her.

Donnay's smile deepened. "Before Valentine's Day. I can't imagine them waiting longer than that. And trust me when I say that this time, she has no qualms leaving here and traveling with Dad, although she'll wait until after Gramps's surgery, of course. She's satisfied that you and I have decided to make our home here and we'll keep an eye on my grandparents. Mom deserves to finally spend time with the man she loves and to be happy."

"You deserve to be happy as well. I love you," he whispered close to her ear.

She smiled at him. "And I love you, too."

She snuggled deeper into the arms she had once believed were incapable of loving anyone, especially her. He had proven her wrong, and every time she looked into his eyes, she saw the truth reflected in their dark depths. He was a man who, she had discovered, not only had a lot of forbidden passion, but also had a lot of hidden talents. She couldn't help wondering where he got some of his smooth moves and creative positions when they made love.

"Ready again?"

She chuckled as she turned in his arms. She couldn't say he hadn't warned her about his inexhaustible energy. Reaching up, she placed her arms around his neck. "For you, Spencer Westmoreland, I'll always be ready."

Epilogue

Spencer stood beside Reggie, the youngest of his brothers, who was still a bachelor and who was standing as his best man. Spencer watched his beautiful bride walk down the aisle to him on her father's arm. He thought Chardonnay was a stunning vision in white. The top of her gown fitted tightly to the waist and then flared out in a thousand ruffles.

All the love he never thought possible was flowing through him at that moment and he definitely couldn't wait for their wedding night. After spending the night in their villa, they would be flying out in the morning for Paris where they would spend two weeks.

"You sure you want to do this?" Reggie asked, leaning over to whisper in his ear.

Spencer grinned, not taking his gaze off Chardonnay. "Hell, yes."

His brother Jared, standing close by as a groomsman, poked him in the ribs, reminding him of the preacher who was within earshot. That didn't bother Spencer. On this day, his wedding day, nothing would bother him.

When Chardonnay reached his side and gave him her hand, he took it and lifted it up to his lips and kissed it. What the hell, he thought. He could definitely do better than that. Then he pulled her into his arms and kissed her lips. She returned his kiss in kind, until a few guests cleared their throats, reminding the couple of their presence.

Spencer pulled back and met the minister's frown. "You're supposed to wait until after I pronounce you husband and wife," the pastor scolded them in a low voice, trying to keep the smile off his face.

Spencer gave the minister a mischievous grin. "I know, sir. I'm sorry. I got carried away."

And then the wedding ceremony began.

When it ended, the minister presented the couple as husband and wife, and Spencer kissed his bride all over again.

* * * * *

Turn the page for a sneak preview
of the first book in the new miniseries
DIAMONDS DOWN UNDER
from Silhouette Desire®,
VOWS & A VENGEFUL GROOM
by Bronwyn Jameson

Available January 2008

Silhouette Desire®
Always Powerful, Passionate and Provocative

Kimberley Blackstone didn't notice the waiting horde of media until it was too late. Flashbulbs exploded around her like a New Year's light show. She skidded to a halt, so abruptly her trailing suitcase all but overtook her.

This had to be a case of mistaken identity. Surely. Kimberley hadn't been on the paparazzi hit list for close to a decade, not since she'd estranged herself from her billionaire father and his headline-hungry diamond business.

But no, it was *her* name they called. *Her* face was the focus of a swarm of lenses that circled her like avid hornets. Her heart started to pound with fear-fueled adrenaline.

What did they want?

What was going on?

With a rising sense of bewilderment she scanned the crowd for a clue, and her gaze fastened on a tall, leonine figure forcing his way to the front. A tall, familiar figure. Her head came up in stunned recognition, and their gazes collided across the sea of heads before the cameras erupted with another barrage of flashes, this time right in her exposed face.

Blinded by the flashbulbs—and by the shock of that momentary eye-meet—Kimberley didn't realize his intent until he'd forged his way to her side, possibly by the sheer strength of his personality. She felt his arm wrap around her shoulder, pulling her into the protective shelter of his body, allowing her no time to object. No chance to lift her hands to ward him off.

In the space of a hastily drawn breath, she found herself plastered knee-to-nose against six feet two inches of hard-bodied male.

Ric Perrini.

Her lover for ten torrid weeks, her husband for ten tumultuous days.

Her ex for ten tranquil years.

After all this time, he should not have felt so familiar but, oh dear, he did. She knew the scent of that body and its lean, muscular strength. She knew its heat and its slick power and every response it could draw from hers.

She also recognized the ease with which he'd taken control of the moment and the decisiveness of his deep voice when it rumbled close to her ear. "I have a car waiting outside. Is this your only luggage?"

Kimberley nodded. "I assume you will tell me," she said tightly, "what this welcome party is all about."

"Not while the welcome party is within earshot. No."

Barking a request for the cameramen to stand aside, Perrini took her hand and pulled her into step with his ground-eating stride. Kimberley let him, because he was right, damn his arrogant, Italian-suited hide. Despite the speed with which he whisked her across the airport terminal, she could almost feel the hot breath of the pursuing media on her back.

This was neither the time nor the place for explanations. Inside his car, however, she would get answers.

Now that the initial shock had been blown away— by the haste of their retreat, by the heat of her gathering indignation, by the rush of adrenaline fired by Perrini's presence and the looming verbal battle—her brain was starting to tick over. This had to be her father's doing. And if it was a Howard Blackstone publicity ploy, then it had to be about Blackstone Diamonds, the company that ruled his life.

The knowledge made her chest tighten with a familiar ache of disillusionment.

She'd known her father would be flying in from Sydney for today's opening of the newest in his chain of exclusive, high-end jewelry boutiques. The opulent shopfront sat adjacent to the rival business where Kimberley worked. No coincidence, she thought bitterly, just as it was no coincidence that Ric Perrini was here in Auckland ushering her to his car.

Perrini was Howard Blackstone's right-hand man, second in command at Blackstone Diamonds, a legacy of his short-lived marriage to the boss's daughter. No doubt her father had sent him to fetch her; the question was *why?*

* * * * *

Get swept away down under with the glitz and glamour of the Blackstone empire as Kimberley tries to determine the real reason behind her "reunion" with Ric....

Look for VOWS & A VENGEFUL GROOM
by Bronwyn Jameson,
in stores January 2008.